This Ever Diverse Pair

Published by Barfield Press

Books by Owen Barfield:

Poetic Diction: A Study in Meaning
Romanticism Comes of Age
This Ever Diverse Pair
Saving the Appearances: A Study in Idolatry
Worlds Apart: A Dialogue of the 1960's
Unancestral Voice
Speaker's Meaning
What Coleridge Thought
The Rediscovery of Meaning and Other Essays
History, Guilt and Habit
Owen Barfield on CS Lewis
Night Operation
Eager Spring
The Rose on the Ash-Heap

Translations:

The Case for Anthroposophy

Forthcoming new editions:

The Silver Trumpet
Orpheus: A Poetic Drama
English People
Short stories
Poetry

www.owenbarfield.org

Owen Barfield

This Ever Diverse Pair

Barfield Press
OXFORD, ENGLAND

Series Editor: Dr. Jane Hipolito.

Published by Barfield Press UK, Oxford, England.

First published by Victor Gollancz, London 1950.
Second edition by Floris Books, Edinburgh 1985.
This third edition by Barfield Press, Oxford 2010.

A catalogue record for this book is available from
the British Library.

This Ever Diverse Pair by Owen Barfield
ISBN 978-0-9559582-5-0

Author photo, Owen Barfield 1973: © 2010 Carol Reck.
All rights reserved.

Translation and footnotes: Dr. Amy Vail and Dr. Jane Hipolito.

Printed on paper with Sustainable Forestry Initiative
(SFI) accreditation.

Produced on behalf of
the Owen Barfield Literary Estate.

The Literary Estate promotes and safeguards the works
and intellectual legacy of Arthur Owen Barfield.

D̊B

www.owenbarfield.org

To

My Long-suffering Partner

— the real one

With the exception of one chapter, which is with permission (and even encouragement) founded irresponsibly on fact, all the events and characters portrayed in this book are entirely imaginary.*

* This chapter is VI. The Things that are Caesar's! which wittily describes how C. S. Lewis ("Ramsden") established a charitable fund with the assistance of his solicitor, Owen Barfield ("Burgeon" and "Burden").

CONTENTS

INTRODUCTION

Frederick J. Dennehy, 2010

OWEN BARFIELD ONCE wrote that while his friend C. S. Lewis "grew" as a writer over the years, there was "no earlier Barfield and no later Barfield. He always says the same thing." Although Barfield was having some fun at his own expense, he was in a sense right. From his early works on etymology and poetic theory to his later philosophical works, Barfield tends to produce variations on a single theme. That theme is polarity.

Samuel Taylor Coleridge, who kindled Barfield's thinking for three quarters of a century, cited Heraclitus as the originator of what he termed the "universal law of polarity." A mere logical paradox, as Coleridge never tired of emphasizing, is static, a standoff, while the polarities of Heraclitus are dynamic. They generate something other than themselves, and in that sense they produce objective knowledge.

Coleridge was the philosopher of polarity. He built immense verbal cathedrals around the subject. In the definition he gave at the beginning of the famous thirteenth chapter of the *Biographia Literaria*, polar opposites are "two contrary forces, the one of which tends to expand infinitely, while the other strives to apprehend or find itself in this infinity." Elsewhere he refers to polarity as "productive unity," "separative projection," and "the tendency at once to individuate and connect, to detach, but so as either to retain or to reproduce attachment." He claimed to have located the beginnings of a "polar logic" in the writings of Giordano Bruno, but apart from the outlines of a scheme involving a diagrammatic relationship featuring Thesis, Antithesis, Synthesis and Prothesis, and some scattered references to what he calls the Principle of Trichotomy, "polar logic" remains, like much of what Coleridge began to rough out during his career, an idea whose time never came.

Barfield, for all his immense respect for Coleridge, recognized the need for clarity. It quickly becomes clear from reading Barfield that polar opposites are not contraries or contradictories on the Aristotelian square of opposition. They are not mutually exclusive. Polarities have none of the solidity of the earth element, in which fixed entities occupy either separate and distinct spaces, or the same space at separate and distinct times, like (to use a favorite illustration of Barfield) "Box and Cox." Polarity belongs more to the watery element, in which opposing forces mix and interpenetrate, like separate currents in a single stream, indivisible but very much distinguishable.

As Barfield tells us in his 1971 essay, "Either: Or," reproduced in the collection *Owen Barfield on C. S. Lewis*, there is a reciprocal relationship within polarity: "The more there is of me the less there is of you." But he insists that polarities exist "by virtue of each other as well as at the expense of each other." His most elaborate simile for polarity is "two nations at total war, each with a network of spies and an effective resistance movement distributed throughout the others' territory — and each with a secret underground passage opening into the citadel in the heart of its enemy's territory."

Philosophers love to resolve opposition. But the whole point of polarity is that the opposition does not go away. Mind and matter, man and nature, conscious and unconscious, subject and object — all remain apart, in tension. We don't ultimately choose one over the other. Nor do we bring them together in a climactic embrace or fusion. Any "resolution of opposites" would mean the disappearance of one through its engulfment by the other, or else a denial of the original opposition through some philosophical or verbal sleight-of-hand. And Barfield will have none of that.

The point of polarity is that the more opposition there is, the more unity there is. Polarity is not abstract, but concrete — in fact, polarity is the very essence of concreteness. As opposed to logical opposites, which exclude each other, polar opposites generate each other, just as the severed head of certain life forms will generate a tail or the severed tail will generate a head. At first only the tension is conscious, but then the unity, which was there all along, becomes conscious as well.

Barfield asks, "In what way is imagination true?" He understands "truth" not as a correspondence with some pre-existing thing, but in the ancient Greek sense of an "unforgetting," an "unconcealment," a revealing of what had been hidden. And polarity yields just that kind of truth. It is not just another variation on the way the poet rearranges a reality that is already "out there." Polarity doesn't reorganize the world, it reveals it, and by revealing it, transforms it for us.

There is a reason why Barfield "always says the same thing." He can never fully explain polarity. Certainly not dialectically. He can only hope to elicit the imagination of polarity in his readers. In re-reading Barfield, one sometimes seems to be encountering him for the first time, as if the words had not been there before or as if he had somehow grown wiser since we last turned the pages. That experience in a reader is usually the signature of imagination in the writer. Because the theme cannot be formulated in a phrase or comprehended in a single reading, there is nothing for us to hold on to, nothing to possess. There is nothing for the ego to feast on.

Barfield himself was too deliberate, too careful and too shrewd a lawyer to allow himself to ignore the consequences of his arguments. His seduction of his readers looked toward a very real consummation. Because Barfield understood that knowing is the equivalent of being, he endeavored not just to introduce his readers to new avenues of thought, but to awaken them to a different order of reality. We should recall (as Barfield candidly acknowledges in his seminal work *Saving the Appearances: A Study in Idolatry*) that an overriding concern for him in most of what he put to paper was to exorcise the taboos against his readers' acceptance of the systematic use of the imagination, the practice of which is found in the anthroposophy of Rudolf Steiner. For this reason, C. S. Lewis recognized that polarity represented an attack on the very basis of his thinking, and he resisted it with every device of logic, wit and common sense in his formidable arsenal. For Lewis, Barfield's easy, friendly, soft-spoken prose disguised a premeditated assault on everything civilized discourse relied upon.

The Law of Contradiction, for one thing. The Law of the Excluded Middle for another. Laws that for Lewis (and for most of us, no doubt) are eternal, are for Barfield only "parochial interludes" in the history of philosophy. Minor distortions of polar logic. Lewis had a visceral aversion to anything that appeared to blur distinctions, or to disrespect the sanctity of the ordained threshold between mind and matter, subject and object, human and divine. The experience of imagination was surely a joy for Lewis, and he lovingly produced it in his fiction, but to elevate imagination to the level of truth seemed to him not only arrogant but dangerous. Open the door of that threshold and who knows what manner of living thing you could let in.

Barfield said in the conversation with Shirley Sugerman that opens her wonderful collection of essays in *Evolution of Consciousness: Studies in Polarity*, that polarity is a paradox in terms of abstract thought, but "a mystery as it begins to be experienced."

"Mystery" is a provocative term to use. One fruitful way of approaching it is by focusing on the very revealing polarity between individuality and universality. As Barfield said to Ms. Sugerman, "you can't really acquire anything that could reasonably be called universal consciousness except by becoming still more individual than you are now. The more individual you become, if it is really individual and not just simply self-centeredness, the more universal you are."

There is no doubt that this polarity is borne out in our experience of the greatest — that is the most universal — artists. As Georg Kuhlewind has pointed out, Johann Sebastian Bach is a brilliant representative of the musical Baroque period, and specifically the German Baroque period, but at the same time his compositions are unmistakably individual. Anyone who knows classical music well cannot fail to recognize him as the composer of a piece after hearing the first few bars. But the individuality of his style in no way limits his universality. In fact, the more individual he is the more Baroque he is, the more German he is, and the more he is a representative of humankind. The same is true of Shakespeare and Rembrandt.

This appears as a paradox to almost everyone who thinks about it. How can what is by definition unique at the same time encompass the whole? We begin, but only begin, to grasp this polarity when we recognize that whatever does not reduce to the past is a creation, and that all creation therefore must inhabit a place of beginning, what the Greeks called *"arche."* *"Arche"* is itself impossible to define, but participation in it demands a change in our way of experiencing from being to becoming, and in thinking from the mirrored past to the living present. This emancipation from what Coleridge called "the lethargy of custom" is not only open to great artists like Bach and Shakespeare and Rembrandt, but to any human being who has the will to interrupt the chain of passive causation in order to choose something new out of freedom. Someone who performs a seemingly inconspicuous gesture that initiates community by bringing persons together, or someone who resists the encrusted habits of years by making an act of forgiveness is a creator. In deeds of creation, of letting go the conditions and causes of the past, the true individual emerges from the personality for the first time. Because every past is unique, every sacrifice of the past has its own style, its own flavor, its own touch, and for that reason is wholly individual. And because every such sacrifice is genuinely creative, it is universal as well.

The universal is not the "general." It cannot be experienced by examining many instances in order to spot what is constant, but only by the kind of change of consciousness Barfield speaks of in *Poetic Diction: A Study in Meaning*. It is not a case of laboriously reducing the many to one. Rather, the one is seen reflected in the many, so that the many are seen in the light of one. The "general" is only what Henri Bortoft has called "the intellectual mind's counterfeit for the universal." In generalizing, as the poet Rumi said, we "name everything according to the number of legs it has." We observe, like Linnaeus, so that we can classify and distinguish, but we ignore *the being* of the things we classify. That being can only be grasped through polarity. But in principle it is accessible to every human being. For that reason it is "universal."

It should hardly be surprising that polarity manifested in Barfield's own life. For a variety of personal reasons, he made his career the law, which is abstract, while his deepest interest, the poetic, is living and organic. Of this polarity of his person, Barfield told Shirley Sugerman candidly that:

> ... being instinctively in the one and being compelled to live with my mind and activity very much in the other did lead, over a great part of my life, I suppose, to a kind of polarity as tension, very much as tension. And the tension at one stage became so violent that, together with other pressures, it very nearly resulted in a nervous breakdown; and I think I've always thought, looking back, that I avoided a nervous breakdown largely by writing that little book *This Ever Diverse Pair* and really in a way I did it out of that impulse, out of desperation, rather than having any hope of ever publishing it as a book. The characters Burden and Burgeon are embodiments or symbols, or whatever, of a very real experience of polarity and tension in my own life.

This Ever Diverse Pair, then, was cathartic. It seems entirely fitting, to those who had the pleasure of knowing Owen Barfield, that what Aristotle defined in his analysis of tragedy, Owen Barfield should enact by way of comedy. And *This Ever Diverse Pair* is certainly comedic. It is at the same time a wry commentary on the legal profession and expansively "humorous" in the Dickensian sense. It seems likely that Barfield's therapeutic result had much to do with the ironic distancing from the treadmill of daily life that he achieved with the marvelous literary device of casting a solicitor's sole proprietorship as a bickering partnership between two very different personae (Burgeon the creative idealist and Burden the meticulously analytical realist). He maintains that device without flinching for more than 100 pages in telling the story of their increasingly tense relationship.

There is much in the law that is prosaic, analytical, habitual and formulaic, and there is little doubt that the constant need to attend to matters on this basis was in large part what precipitated the crisis in Barfield's life. But unless Burgeon (the creative, expansive side of the practice) and Burden (the critical, minutiae-oriented part of the practice) work together — and actually generate each other's "genius" — the practice fails.

Even with the separation of 60 years and a (to me) foreign form of practice, it is astonishing how many of this book's anecdotal chapters are so recognizable to an American lawyer. Clients, courts, practitioners and situations don't vary all that much. What Barfield brings to this litany of legal vicissitudes, however, is a genuine concern, even a tenderness, for everyone who plays a part.

Barfield notes on the flyleaf of this book that "with the exception of one chapter, which is with permission (and even encouragement) founded irresponsibly on fact, all the events and characters portrayed in this book are entirely imaginary." The chapter to which Barfield refers is VI, "The Things That Are Caesar's!," which presents an undisguised portrait of both his legal and his personal relationship with C. S. Lewis. I recognized, on re-reading this book, that my impression of Lewis's personality has been largely formed by this chapter. It is a gem. Lewis was beloved as a friend, but given his low tolerance for the practical and worldly, somewhat challenging as a client. Incidentally, the intellectual relationship between

Barfield and Lewis, often referred to as the "Great War," was itself a paradigmatic polarity.

Yet another polarity — that between Law and Equity — emerges brilliantly in a dream sequence near the end of the book. The equity courts (which assumed a powerful position in English jurisprudence shortly after the time of Shakespeare), were originally "courts of conscience," and acted with reference to the person rather than to abstract "rights." As Barfield recognized in his insightful 1932 essay "Equity", conscience means "knowing with," and is both an act of will and the basis of self-consciousness. As *This Ever Diverse Pair* draws to a close, equity is rediscovered as the "heart" of the profession, so often hidden in practice by the "lethargy of custom."

Equity, in Anglo-American jurisprudence is applicable exclusively to civil causes. But Barfield imagines a form of equity in the criminal sphere that anticipates, obliquely but provocatively, the reconciliation tribunals operating in Africa and elsewhere today that may eventually reshape the criminal justice systems of tomorrow.

It is perhaps not too much to hope that, with its scrupulously honest look at the experience of dissonance in the practice of the profession and its keen focus on the personal meaning of justice, *This Ever Diverse Pair* is a book for our own time. For anyone with a taste for fiction that is fresh and original, it will be a joy. For practicing lawyers, it should be kept on the table next to the bed — or perhaps in the medicine cabinet.

FOREWORD

Walter De La Mare, 1950

WITHOUT THE FAINTEST desire to trespass into the private lives of one's fellow creatures — a sort of *tort*, rampant it would seem, in the whole world's newspapers — one yet cannot but wonder at times what is involved, in the way of personal experience, in their *less* private lives. What, for example, is it really 'like' to be a Dictator, a Field Marshal, a dignitary of the Church, a Merchant Prince, a demagogue, an 'eminent' surgeon, a Functionary — or, for that matter, the local grocer, a midwife, a Sister of Mercy, the public hangman or the village blacksmith. What does any such order of existence *mean* to one? Especially when one is alone? What, in these strange, alien circumstances, is one likely to have to face, to ponder on, disentangle, imagine, put up with, resent? Even get away with; find peace in? — grievances, ambitions, enticements, dangers, ruling passions, rewards? How does one manage to keep the two kinds of existence in concord and tranquillity one with the other. And in relation to the open secrets and the hidden deeps? Are we all, to quote our author, thus "constantly finding" ourselves, as he finds himself, "involved in small but apparently insoluble moral problems"?

One of the many fascinating rewards of his book is that, in its profoundly serious yet light-hearted fashion, it repeatedly casts a piercing though indirect beam of light on practically every other office, occupation and profession by irradiating his own — that of the Law. And for most of us, the Law is not only a dread and Sealed Book, but one which, when it is opened, proves to be largely unintelligible. The Law... Never, never — solemnly adjured me two sagacious legal friends of years and years ago — never, never go to it!

Let it be said at once that Mr. Burgeon is not precisely what one expects a solicitor to be: formal, discreet, cautious, reticent, prosy, perfervidly practical, devoted to and flawlessly proud of his profession:

> Discreet he was, and of greet reverence:
> He semed swich, his wordes weren so wyse ...
> Al was fee simple to him in effect
> His purchasing mighte nat been infect.
> No-wher so bisy a man as he ther nas,
> And yet he semed bisier than he was ...[1]

But this was in Geoffrey Chaucer's fragrant day, when it was nothing unusual for cited Law to go back to the Conqueror. Times seem to have changed. And nothing is more surprising in the surprising chapters that follow that Mr. Burgeon is seldom actually any of these things and never all of them together. He is so natural, and seems to be so much 'one of us' that you might suppose he would be equally terrified at sight of a policeman at the front door and hardly able to whisper in the presence of a Judge. As in fact, in spite of exquisite provocation, he fails to do in his last chapter. He is at least as conscientious as a poet — since he is a poet himself; and he not only

---

[1] Chaucer, *The Canterbury Tales*, General Prologue 312–13, 319–22.

quotes Greek and German verse, but his own — which, for this purpose, is usually in forcible terms.

Nor is there the least need to take any of these surprises, and many others, with a grain of salt. Truth alone will preserve almost anything from putrefaction. And a hatred of sham, a love of Nonsense, and the refusal to be a 'Lynx' or a 'Glossy' must be a sovereign help in keeping anything sweet — even the Law. Besides, he not only wears a very likeable bowler and an entirely trustworthy grin, "about halfway between Mona Lisa and the Cheshire Cat", but has obviously lived and flourished so long among the best words in the best order (for rational *and* imaginative purposes) in an English dictionary that now, having not the least need of any, he can *write*. And that ability in practice (besides doubling the Burden!) implies the lifelong endeavour to keep one's mind lucid, faithful to itself, free from sham, and one's own.

Alas, our friend Burgeon has a partner. Not wholly by chance, it would seem, he is named Burden. Not wholly by chance, perhaps, neither partner is given a christian name. It is they who are 'this ever diverse pair', this two-in-one, victims of that mental and moral and ethical dualism which haunts, afflicts, vitalizes, and indeed humanizes poor humanity, great and small: the Box's and Cox's, the Jekylls and Hydes of every tint and tinge, the children of grace and of wrath, the little Conservatives and Communists, N. *and* M. Or, as the title of a once much-loved Victorian romance put it: *We Two*. And Messrs. Burden and Burgeon are in a partnership closer even that that of the Siamese twins.

They share the same table in the same office, the same telephone; are both of them up to their eyes in the Law. They argue and quarrel in it. It is on these occasions that Burden, from being formal, sober, stringently business-like — that domino of many colours — is apt to become infantinely serio-comic, and Burgeon in deadly and yet life-giving earnest. It is Burgeon, none the less, though never bird or wild flower desecrates his parchment cell, who has the humour and good-humour, the 'nature', the balance and faith, the *style* of mind, spirit and inkwell which will transport with ease even as desperately befogged a reader as I was, through the Oakeshott-Meering's unspeakable Abstract of Title, to "that extraordinary chap, Ramsden", to the guileless little remainderman, on to such dreams as *Alice through the Looking-Glass* is made on, and so, finally to this diverse pair's bitter-sweet Judgment day. And that is the least foreseen and the most beguiling surprise (and reconciliation) of all.

It would be difficult to say what has given me the most pleasure and enlightenment in this book: its novelty and richness, its humour (sweet and 'dry'), its imaginativeness, the poise of its gravity, or the company of half the 'pair'.

This Ever Diverse Pair

ἐγώ γὰρ διὰ νόμου νόμῳ ἀπέθανον ...[1]
ὁ γὰρ νόμος ὀργὴν κατεργάζεται ...[2]
ἀλλὰ τὴν ἁμαρτίαν οὐκ ἔγνων εἰ μὴ διὰ νόμου.[3]

For I through the law am dead to the law ...
Because the law worketh wrath ...
Nay, I had not known sin, but by the law.
                    St. Paul's Epistles to the Galatians and the Romans

Thus piteously Love closed what he begat:
The union of this ever-diverse pair!
                                        George Meredith, *Modern Love*

[1] Galatians 2:19, King James Version.
[2] Romans 4:15, KJV.
[3] Romans 7:7, KJV.

I
TABULA IN NAUFRAGIO[1]

OF COURSE HE already keeps a diary in a sense, like any other solicitor — a great fat thing bound in coloured boards and buff leather, which looks rather like a sporting bible and doesn't tell you anything about him. What it does tell you about is costs, stamp duties, the names and addresses of other solicitors and the formalities preceding cremation. All this is in very small print, while the blank pages of the diary proper contain laconic and virtually illegible pencil entries of the nature of "10.30 Mackenzie Summons" or "Mrs. Parsons" or simply "15/2"; with a sprinkling of occasional intimacies like "Call for G's shoes" or just "toffee".

If this partner of mine kept a real diary, there would be no need to write all this about him. As it is, you can take it that *this* is his, or rather our, true diary — in exactly what sense will appear, I hope, as it proceeds. It will certainly not be a diary in common form.

[1] Legal Latin. Lit. a plank in a shipwreck. The reference is to Cicero, *De Officiis* 3.89: *Si tabulam de naufragio stultus arripuerit extorquebitne eam sapiens si potuerit.* (In a shipwreck, if a fool snatches a plank, should not a wise man take it away from him if he can?) The phrase *tabula in naufragio* has been interpreted to mean *a court of last resort.* It is often preceded by *res ipsa loquitur* (the matter speaks for itself.) This refers to cases in which a lender invests in a property or part of a property, not knowing that the property in question already has two mortgages on it. By joining his claim to that of the first lender, he unfairly manages to end up with the lion's share.

But first let me make it quite clear that I am not writing it out of any love of the man. Quite the reverse, in spite of our long and close connection. I am doing it simply because I must now write about something or die. If I *do* die — but we will come to that later. I would much rather write about something else, but, as a painter can paint only what he can see, and, if there is something which girdles and confines his entire horizon, must paint that or nothing, so a writer, if there is somebody who exacts his unremitting attention during waking hours, must either write about that somebody or hold his peace.

Over and over again I have started writing about something really interesting or useful — classical stuff, matters of public interest, the Lord knows what — only to be pulled up with a jerk. Just as I am getting absorbed in it, up comes Burden. "Hi!" he says. "I want you! You must stop that!" I stop with a wrench and an abiding grudge against him. And when five or six weeks later there is a chance to start again, I shrink from re-absorption — remembering the wrench. You can't really write with any force about anything on which you are never allowed to fix your attention. But the only thing on which I am allowed, and indeed expected, to fix my attention, is Burden. So I am writing about him.

Let me do him justice. It was *my* doing that we ever went into the law at all. I, Burgeon, am responsible for the present constitution of the firm of Burden and Burgeon. I am responsible for the professional existence, almost for the existence at all, of Burden. I deliberately called him forth from his obscurity — summoned him, as it were, from the realm of the Mothers[2], and set him up in space and time. It is not the fault of either of us that we have since become involved in a complex of responsibilities from which there may be no way out until the shadows lengthen, the busy world is hushed and our work is done. It may not be the fault of either of us — it is certainly not his — that he is turning into a sort of Frankenstein. But in all my present bewilderment I am at least certain of this: that if, without injuring anyone but him, I can do anything to arrest the process and keep my own end up, I ought to do it. So I am going to try keeping his diary, and see what happens.

This is my declaration of independence. I always thought I should be able to keep that, but now I am afraid. The original idea was, that he was to earn the bread and butter and I was to support him as a sleeping partner. I was to put in exactly as much *time* at the office as he did, but nothing much else; and in my spare time I was to carry on as before. I admit I also had the ineffable idea that, I being (at any rate by inclination) a poet and he a business man, the association might in some undefined way work out for the benefit of both poetry in general and business in general, and thereby contribute to the gaiety of nations and the amelioration of society. (Romeo and Juliet were to do as much for the Montagues and Capulets.) But this wasn't the essence of the contract; alternatively it hasn't worked, there is a total failure of consideration, the contract is frustrated and under the

---

[2] Goethe's Faust goes to the realm of the Mothers to fetch the ghost of Helen of Troy. (*Faust* 2.6229)

Law Reform (Frustrated Contracts) Act 1943 I am under no obligation to him of any sort whatever.

How could we possibly foresee that in 1931, less than six months after we joined forces, the pervasive strain on the whole economic system would begin, that it would get tenser and tenser until it culminated in the War, that life in a solicitor's office would be like life in an understaffed telephone exchange? It was quiet enough, at least in externals, fifty years ago, I am told. How could I have foreseen that by 1941 both the other members of the firm would be *hors de combat* and we two, inadequately equipped with experience, still half green, carrying on the whole business alone? Take a Rugby football player, knowing the rules of the game well enough, having learnt it well at school, having perhaps played once or twice for his college (notwithstanding a slight lameness in one leg); drop him by parachute into the middle of the scrum at an International Match, informing him casually, as you press the release-button, that he is captain of his side: he will have an idea of our position.

It is odd to reflect that only a few years ago I made a stern and deliberate resolve to abandon all writing on personal subject-matter. It seemed to me, and it still seems, that this particular romantic vein is thoroughly worked out. I don't like it even when the raw material is transmuted into first-rate lyric. True, many of the poems which have given me the keenest pleasure are made of it. The best of the few lyrics which I myself have put up were all of this type, written to relieve my personal griefs and in fact relieving them. That made no difference. It began to disgust me. I wanted, above all, to be objective, to write about Nature and events and quite other people, using my own feelings solely as instruments of perception and fountains of diction, sacrificing them like the glass in the window, to let in the light and the warmth of the outside world. And now here I am, at it again!

The whole trouble is that the sleeping partner doesn't get enough sleep. I don't mind having to be in Burden's room while he is doing his work. I expected that. After all, I am invisible, and no one else knows I am there. (At least, I imagine not.) As long as he is jogging away at routine work without interruptions, I would as lief be there as in any other place where I am not allowed to be actually about either my own or my Father's business. What I object to is the unexpected degree of *attention* he demands. I can't call it exertion. If it were, it mightn't be so bad. But in practice there is very little routine work without interruption, and every time he is interrupted he calls for me. Every time the telephone bell rings, *I* have to answer it, ascertain who is there and what he is talking about, and then, if I am lucky, I can hand over to Burden. The systematic 'waking' of witches in the Middle Ages is usually referred to by modern historians as just an instance of barbarous torture. I don't believe the infliction of pain was the main object of this procedure — which involved the systematic prevention of sleep for days at a time by pins, pinches or other light nervous shocks. The object, and the necessary object, was to keep the other part of the woman *there*; I mean the sleeping partner who had other things to do in her spare time, and who perhaps

would have been off on the very mischief they were
seeking to prevent if they had merely used the rack.

> Was it a *hundred* times today
> I nodded and began to sway,
> Drowsed, and the blank walls dropped away?
>
> Faces and voices merge; the glare
> Softens to dusk; the live black air
> Bosoms me: *Whisk! My broomstick there!* —
>
> *Hey up the chimney!* — sharp the pin
> Of gaoler jerks me back to skin: —
> "Pardon me, is your *partner* in?"

Worst of all, I find that nearly all *decisions* have to be
made by me. And this part of the work is not even
confined to office hours. He tells me to take them home
with me and (the supreme imposition) to *use my imagination*!
Why on earth should imagination be necessary for these
fiddling problems? And then there are the awful times
when he is so tired that I have to keep *him* awake!

Of course, someone will say that all this is a subtle
form of exhibitionism or narcissism or some nastyism or
other. It might be if I were writing to please others. But in
point of fact it's a matter of complete — well, almost
complete — indifference whether anybody else ever
reads it or not. I am doing it for my own salvation.
Burden is eating me up, my time, my wit, my memory,
my 'shaping spirit of imagination', my whole *me*. Take
poetry, for instance. The other evening he was so exhausted
and spiritless and devoid of hope that he asked me to
write a poem about *his* feelings. That's the sort of thing he

does — calls on me to exert the very abilities he is destroying. I produced the following quatrain for him: —

> How I hate this bloody business,
> Peddling property and strife
> While the pulse of Europe falters —
> How I hate this bloody life!

And he paid me the last insult of *praising* it. He thought it was good. In fact the silly ass was so pleased with it that he kept saying it over and over again to himself, in the train going home, till he fell asleep and overshot his station!

It may be that there is some impropriety, or even danger, in writing about anyone as closely connected with me as Burden is. So close that, until twelve months ago, I had never even dreamed about him. As I hesitated, pen in hand, before I began to write all this — pondering the very doubts I am now trying to express — my mind went back to that perhaps prophetic dream. I was sitting at a concert in a full hall, when I caught a glimpse of him walking down the middle, looking along the rows for a vacant seat that wasn't there. In my dream it was a second or two before I established the identity of that intelligent, anxious, tolerably ugly face under the bowler hat, though I know it well enough, and the moment I had done so, I woke up — feeling a little frightened. It hasn't happened again. Frightened or not, I have got to try some remedy beyond those I have tried already, and the homeopathic one is the only one that suggests itself. A hair of the dog that bites me. Kill or cure. Perhaps it may be cure, for, to be honest, I feel a bit better already.

II

GRADUATED COURTESIES

"Hooray!" said Burden, as we were opening the post this morning. "There's a cheque in from Holdon. By return of post, too. Beyond all hopes!"

"Any letter with it?" I asked.

I was curious to know what had happened to this man. He was one of those meteoric, or rather comet-like clients, who appear out of space, recommended by some friend to whom they have confided their spot of trouble, and disappear into it again as soon as their matter is done. This one had not been seen at our office for the last nine months. It had been a trifling affair, and we had forgotten to bill him — partly because we never knew whether the job was finished or not.

No. There was no letter, it seemed: just the account we had sent him and a cheque with it. Instead of getting on with the morning's work, I got out the bundle and began re-reading the Minutes and Correspondence:

Feb. 13th. Attending you on your calling with Mr. Loggerhead, when after a short heated discussion it was agreed that the latter had better instruct separate solicitors and he left, after which you gave us particulars of the circumstances in which the Company, *Loggerholds Ltd.*, had been formed; Mr Loggerhead providing most of the capital, while you actually ran the Company and did all the work; also of the friendly personal relations which had subsisted between you until a few days ago, and further that Mr. Loggerhead's share-certificate was in the Company's safe, of which you possessed the only key.

Feb. 14th. Attending you on your ringing up informing us that Mr. Loggerhead had instructed Messrs. Pauncefoot & Mecklenburgh and we were to do our best to arrange an amicable settlement on favourable terms.

Feb. 14th, 19 —

Messrs. Pauncefoot & Mecklenburgh.

Dear Sirs,

We have been instructed by Mr. Holdon in the matter of the unfortunate differences which have arisen between himself and Mr. Loggerhead, for whom we understand you act. May we say that it was on our advice that Mr. Loggerhead instructed separate solicitors, as it is our experience that matters of this sort, where there is considerable personal animosity, are more easily adjusted by that means than by direct dealings between the parties.

We are pleased to hear that he has taken our advice and also, if we may say so, that he has selected a firm with which we recollect pleasant relations extending over a period almost longer than we care to compute!

If you will be good enough to telephone us and suggest an appointment, we shall be happy to call on you at your office, when the whole matter can be discussed and no doubt a settlement of the present rather acute differences of opinion between our respective clients can be arrived at on lines satisfactory to both parties.

Yours faithfully,

BURDEN & BURGEON.

Feb. 17th.   Attending Mr. Pauncefoot at the offices of Messrs. Pauncefoot & Mecklenburgh, discussing the whole matter at great length, and on Mr. P. pressing for the return of the share-certificate before any further negotiations should take place, as to which we agreed to take your instructions.

Feb 18th.   Attending you on the telephone reporting yesterday's interview with Mr. Pauncefoot and on your informing us that you would not part with the share-certificate in any circumstances whatever, whether or no we thought there would be any advantage to you in retaining it, and we were to take no further step unless we heard from the other side.

Feb. 28th, 19 —

Messrs. Burden & Burgeon.
  Dear Sirs,

Loggerholds Ltd
Mr. Loggerhead & Mr. Holdon

When our Mr. Pauncefoot had the pleasure of meeting your Mr. Burden on the 17th inst. you will recollect it was agreed between us that, before the terms of a settlement of this matter could be discussed in detail, your Client should return to our Client the share-certificate which is at present in your Client's possession. We feel sure you will advise your Client that this should now be done, in order that the matter may proceed without undue delay and on a more pleasant footing.

Yours faithfully,
PAUNCEFOOT & MECKLENBURGH.

March 2nd, 19 —

Messrs. Pauncefoot & Mecklenburgh.

Dear Sirs,

Loggerholds Ltd

Mr. Holdon & Mr. Loggerhead

We duly received your letter of the 28th ult., for which we thank you. As arranged at our interview on the 17th ult., we have obtained our Client's instructions on your Client's proposal that the share-certificate should be delivered to him. We are afraid our Client does not see that any useful purpose would be served by his parting with the share-certificate (which is his property) at this stage.

Yours faithfully,

BURDEN & BURGEON.

March 3rd, 19 —

Messrs. Burden & Burgeon.

Dear Sirs,

Mr. Loggerhead & Mr. Holdon

We duly received your letter of yesterday's date. We thought we had made it clear at our interview that the share-certificate to which we refer is in our Client's name and evidences his title to the shares in Loggerholds Ltd. which he purchased on the formation of that Company. Accordingly we repeat the request contained in our letter of the 28th ult.

Yours faithfully,

PAUNCEFOOT & MECKLENBURGH.

March 5th, 19 —

Messrs. Pauncefoot & Mecklenburgh.

Dear Sirs,

Without Prejudice

Mr. Holdon and Mr. Loggerhead

In reply to your letter of the 3rd inst. we agree that the share-certificate is in your Client's name. According to our instructions however no shares were in fact allotted, nor does your Client's name appear on the Register of Members of the Company. The certificate (which in our view is a piece of paper of no particular value) was expressly presented by your Client to our Client as a mark of the complete confidence which your Client at that time reposed in him.

Yours faithfully,

BURDEN & BURGEON.

March 6th, 19 —

Messrs. Burden & Burgeon.

Dear Sirs,

Without Prejudice

Mr. Loggerhead & Mr. Holdon

We duly received your letter of the 5th inst., the contents of which amaze us. If your Client persists in his preposterous contention (which we can hardly imagine him to have raised on the advice of your good selves), we are instructed to take such steps as may be necessary to bring him to his senses.

Yours faithfully,

PAUNCEFOOT & MECKLENBURGH.

March 7th, 19 —

Messrs. Pauncefoot & Mecklenburgh.

Dear Sirs,

Mr. Holdon & Mr. Loggerhead

In reply to your letter of yesterday (the tone of which we rather deplore), we have nothing to add to our letter of the 5th inst. except that the advice which we have given or refrained from giving to our Client would appear to be a matter for ourselves.

Yours faithfully,

Burden & Burgeon.

March 9th, 19 —

Messrs. Burden & Burgeon.

Dear Sirs,

Mr. Loggerhead & Mr. Holdon

We have your letter of the 7th inst. We should have thought a firm of repute would have hesitated before acting on instructions of the nature of those which you appear to have received. Will you please inform your Client that the share-certificate must be delivered up in seven days, if proceedings are to be avoided? We shall be prepared to call at your office for it on short appointment by telephone.

Yours faithfully,

Pauncefoot & Mecklenburgh.

March 10th, 19 —

Messrs. Pauncefoot & Mecklenburgh.

Dear Sirs,

Holdon & Loggerhead

We are in receipt of your letter of yesterday's date, the first part of which we consider to be a piece of gratuitous impertinence. As to the second part, we have already informed you that we have nothing to add to our letter of the 5th inst.

Yours faithfully,

BURDEN & BURGEON.

March 11th, 19 —

Messrs. Burden & Burgeon.

Dear Sirs,

Loggerhead & Holdon

This correspondence is becoming distasteful to us. If the share-certificate is not returned by the 17th inst., together with an undertaking by your Client to file a Return of the Allotment and register our Client as a member of the Company within 14 days thereafter, we are instructed to institute immediate proceedings against your Client in detinue for the recovery of the Certificate and against the Company for rectification of the Register by the inclusion of our Client's name as the holder of 200 shares. Please let us know if you will accept service on behalf of Mr. Holdon and the Company respectively.

Yours faithfully,

PAUNCEFOOT & MECKLENBURGH.

March 11th. Attending you on the telephone informing you of our correspondence with Messrs. Pauncefoot & Mecklenburgh and advising you that in our opinion you had no defence to the threatened proceedings and on your instructing us not to give way an inch on any account, as Loggerhead was a cunning so-and-so.

March 12th, 19 —

Messrs. Pauncefoot & Mecklenburgh.

Dear Sirs,

Holdon & Loggerhead

We acknowledge receipt of your letter of yesterday's date. Our own distaste for this correspondence (in which you have twice animadverted on our presumed relations with our Client) is of a less recent growth that yours appears to be. We may add that we are seriously considering placing the whole of it before the Law Society.

Meanwhile you may take it that we will accept service of any proceedings your Client may be foolish enough to bring.

Yours faithfully,

Burden & Burgeon.

And there it ended. We heard no more from Messrs. Pauncefoot & Mecklenburgh. We heard nothing from Holdon. Whether they made it up; whether Loggerholds Ltd. (a company which exists, according to its Memorandum of Association, for a surprising variety of objects including (inter alia) "the construction of sewers, reservoirs, dams, bridges and waterworks", but exists in fact — as everyone who ever had anything to do with it knows perfectly well — for the sole purpose of marketing little pellets of concentrated glue) is still trading or has gone out of business, we do not know. It may be that, on the point of issuing proceedings, Messrs. Pauncefoot & Mecklenburgh mentioned (for the first time) the question of costs, and that both they and their client thereupon received an unpleasant shock. Burden and I know these shocks. Anyway, we never heard another word from anybody till this morning.

The day before yesterday Burden wrote Holdon a polite note, presuming that there was nothing further we could do in this matter, and *therefore* (there is always some excellent reason — apart from simply wanting the money) enclosing a note of our charges. The result now lay before me on the table.

Needless to say, the correspondence was *not* laid before the Law Society, who quite properly would not have taken the slightest interest in it if it had been. Burden and Pauncefoot avoided one another for a few weeks if they happened to meet in the street or the Courts, at first from animosity and then, I think, from an awkward shame at having unwittingly allowed themselves to become infected by their clients' ill temper. (This nuisance happens sometimes. There seems no way of ruling it quite out.) And then even this aftermath disappeared. Burden's face no longer means "Holdon" to Pauncefoot when he sees it, and Pauncefoot's face no longer means "Loggerhead" to Burden. They have forgotten all about it. I propose to do the same.

III

DIVORCE (UNDEFENDED)

THE TELEPHONE BELL rang: "Mrs. ——'s here, Sir."

"See her in a minute."

Burden put the receiver down. He always says and does this whether he is ready or not, and it always faintly irritates me. It's not done to impress the client. Either he wants a minute to make sure that I am there, or else it's simply in order to put off seeing anybody as long as possible, even if only another minute. I'm not sure which. At any rate a minute later he lifted the receiver again:

"Show Mrs. —— in," he said, and I got his smile ready for him, as the steps came along the passage.

Enter Mrs. ——, smartly dressed, attractive in a made-up sort of way and entirely self-assured. Burden began to get her story, and I noted with relief (*a*) that she was not going to be the voluble sort and (*b*) that it was a straightforward adultery. Cruelty and desertion are generally frightful. There is always a muddle, and I have to help him. I have spent literally hours with him and the client, building up a laborious Petition out of ten years' sulks and a couple of slaps, or a desertion out of the sort of aimless drifting apart (to the undisguised satisfaction of both parties) in which — what? — twenty to thirty or how many per cent of twentieth-century middle-class English marriages disappear. When she produced the hotel bill, my satisfaction was complete. There was nothing more for me to do, and I settled down to watch or sleep as I might feel inclined.

Burden was pleased, too, as it transpired at an early stage that the husband had a good salary and stood in no danger of losing it as a result of the proceedings. There are still jobs which are not open to men who have been divorced by their wives. The theory is that it shows a weakness of character or a low standard of morality. I am not sure about the ethics of this, but I have a strong feeling that it must be right because of the kind of people it makes angry.

He took the usual particulars — short history of the marriage, principal addresses of cohabitation, incomes of both parties, payments made by the husband since they separated, and property. All the furniture belonged to the husband, so no squabbling about three-quarters of a sofa. No children, so no bother about custody and no grave exchanges between two old-established firms in the matter of a rocking-horse and a golliwog — not the one which we understand was given to the child by his aunt, but the one which our client purchased for him on his last birthday. The man had even had the sense to place himself in the hands of a decent firm, who had (through him) put her up to bringing the necessary photograph. Service of the Petition could take place at their office. Thanks to her having a tolerable memory and a mind capable of arranging facts in some kind of order, Burden's notes were, for once, coherent, legible and adequate.

Lastly the Discretion Statement — "Have you committed any matrimonial offence? The Petition will have to disclose that, you know." Eyebrows raised. "I mean, have you committed adultery yourself?" Mrs. —— smiled. It was clear that she thought it a funny word to use outside a book. I also saw the faint — very faint — stab to her self-respect and heard its effects in the imperceptible excess of ease with which she replied. This nearly always happens the first time. The honourable Christian husband or wife in the soul dies very comfortably without a struggle, but it still does not like hearing the death-sentence formally pronounced.

"Of *course!*" said Mrs. ——, "you don't suppose I was going to, etc., etc., etc."

Burden shrugged his shoulders, mumbled something about her being, no doubt, quite entitled to take that view of the matter, took particulars, asked if they intended to marry and expressed fatherly approval when he heard that they did.

"Look here, Burden," I said. "You really oughtn't to let it go as easily as that, ὁ γὰρ ἀκούων ὑπομένει ταῦτα καὶ ποιεῖν δοκεῖ,[1] you know. A man may be considered to *do* a thing he lets himself be told of without protesting. Why can't I really talk to her? It's her business, of course, and she may be right; but that doesn't absolve us from putting it to her squarely. At all events you don't mind my casually alluding to the fact that: –

---

[1] This is a translation into Greek, possibly Barfield's own, of the familiar legal maxim *qui tacet consentire videtur* (whoever is silent is considered to be consenting, commonly stated as *silence gives consent*). While the language is strongly reminiscent of Plato's diction in the *Euthyphro* and *Crito*, dialogues Barfield knew well, the maxim itself was originally formulated by Pope Boniface VIII, *Decretals, Liber Sextus*, 5.12.43.

> Love is not love
> Which alters when it alteration finds
> Or bends with the remover to remove?"[2]

"Don't be an ass!" said Burden. "*Look* at her. I needn't say listen to her — you've been doing it already for the last half-hour (I hope). She'd merely think you were an intolerable prig, and I'm not sure she wouldn't be right. And, incidentally, she'd very likely take her business elsewhere."

I looked at the red lips, the shaped, artificial eyebrows, crossing the plucked originals greasy under their absorbent powder, and held my peace — as I always do. Burden told her that it would cost her sixty or seventy pounds and he would want ten pounds on account against disbursements, but that she ought to get most of it back from her husband.

I watched him shake hands and show her out of the room with words of reassurance and comfort.

Everything seemed to go right. Easy service, an adequate order for alimony pending suit, a complacent hotel proprietor, and an intelligent chambermaid. The Lists were light, and the suit came on for hearing in two or three months. Burden went along to the Court himself, as he was a trifle anxious about the 'discretion' evidence and thought that Counsel might need prompting or checking at the psychological moment; but it turned out to have been quite unnecessary. The case was seventh in

[2] Shakespeare's Sonnet 116.

the List, and there were fifteen more to follow it. Burden's Counsel had been conducting the previous case also, and he got his Petitioner into the box before the other Solicitors had finished getting their papers together. Lipstick reduced for the occasion at Burden's suggestion as a prudent concession to the stuffiness of British Themis[3]. Counsel led her at breakneck speed through the brief history of the union. "And was your marriage happy at first?" Yes, it had been. "After that, did you notice a change in his manner and were your suspicions aroused?" And so on to the end. Then the hotel register and the chambermaid. Yes, she remembered the name quite well. Double bed, morning tea and the grand chain.

The Judge: "You must see a great many people coming and going at your hotel every week. Are you quite sure you would recognize these two?"

Chambermaid (conscientiously remembering her proof): "Yes, I particularly remember this couple because they knocked the tea-tray over by accident and broke one of the cups. I had to report it."

I saw the slightly increased alertness of the Judge as he observed to himself that the Solicitors had no doubt put one of them up to that. But the alertness subsided without anything being said, and I knew we were home.

The husband's photograph was handed up to the witness. Yes. That was the gentleman.

---

[3] Themis is the tutelary deity presiding over law-courts. For the phrase "British Themis," Barfield may have been thinking of Milton's Sonnet 21, "To Cyriack Skinner."

Counsel (pointing to the Petitioner with subdued Euclidean triumph): "Was that the lady?"

Chambermaid: "No, Sir!"

Counsel: "Thank you. My Lord, on these facts I ask for, etc., etc., etc."

The Judge: "Yes, Mr. ——"

I saw Burden look at his watch as he held the swing door of the Court open for the client and passed through after her. Seven minutes exactly.

"That's an undefended divorce case, that was!" he said, with one of my smiles.

The lady was in a very good humour too, and they found time for a mutually congratulatory sherry at the Bodega — two, in fact.

I never liked Burden less that I did during those drinks. After lunch, as it was a bright, sunny day, I got him to walk through the ruins of the Temple down to the river. He was fidgeting all the time to get back to the Office, terrified of the afternoon rush, but I managed to hold him there for a little, and we leaned on the embankment wall looking at the river and talking.

Burgeon: "How do these Divorce Judges manage to stand twenty Undefended Cases a day, two or three days a week? It would drive me completely crackers in six months."

Burden (dully): "I don't know. It's their job. They have the Long Vacation."

Burgeon: "Why do these people bother to *marry*? That's what I can't understand."

Burden: "Don't ask me."

Burgeon: "There's no law against fornication *tout simple*. Why do they go to all this expense and trouble for the privilege of being allowed to call it marriage?"

Burden: "Mph."

Burgeon: "It isn't as if there were even any stigma — except in the narrow circle where a stigma also attaches to easy divorce. Do you really think all this dignified language and machinery with the full flavour of the ecclesiastical courts about it ought to be burlesqued over these farmyard readjustments? Isn't it dangerous even legally?"

Burden (gruffly): "It's an abuse of the whole process of the Court. Everyone knows it. 'Farmyard readjustments' is too strong. Must get back to the Office."

Burgeon: "Oh, not just yet! Another five minutes won't make any difference. Look at the sunlight on the river! If you half-shut your eyes and look *at* it, it looks as if the sky were raining stars. They keep breaking and forming up and breaking again on the surface of the water. What was I saying? Incidentally, divorce is about the one thing on which *He* really did lay down definite, categorical rules. And, what's more, it was divorce *a mensa et thoro*[4] — judicial separation — that He forbade. Divorce *a vinculo matrimonii*[5] appears to have been too inconceivable to Him to need even mentioning."

Burden: "I know. This isn't a Christian Society."

---

[4] Legal Latin. Lit. "from the table and bed", signifying a decree of legal seperation.
[5] Legal Latin. Lit. "from the bond of wedlock."

Burgeon: "I thought the War was supposed to be on precisely because it is! Anyway, it's a pretty way of earning a living and supporting a family!"

Burden: "Oh, shut up! For God's sake leave me alone. Just when things are going comfortably for once and there's been nothing to worry about — no jerks — you must start muscling in and pulling this ethical stuff. Go on looking at the river. Why don't you write a poem about it? That's your job. You would have done once — or tried to. Must get back to the Office."

Burgeon: "What you *really* want me to write is not about the river at all, but doggerel about you and your troubles. And you get jolly cross if I try anything else. You know how much time and attention it absorbs, and that it's a breach of the 'whole time and attention' clause in the Partnership Agreement. You've often told me so yourself."

Burden: "Oh, hell!"

Burgeon: "Don't be cross! I'll try a sort of compromise, if you like — one stanza for me and one for you."

Burden: "Do what you like! Must get back to the Office."
I did try: –

TEMPLE
(Solicitor's Song)

Burgeon: The little waves on London River
                Are bombed with light: they flash and quiver
                And laugh and toss back to the Giver
                His shattered shards. They dance their dance.

Burden: I dance my dance too in that station
To which He called me — litigation
To gild the tide of fornication,
Leases, and lusts, and loan-finance.

IV

ABSTRACT OF THE TITLE

"ARE YOU ATTENDING?"

Well, she hadn't been, of course. But really it was very
difficult — difficult to understand and difficult to keep
her mind on it, even if she *had* understood. She wondered
why Papa had suddenly spoken in that horrid sharp voice.
He had been so good-humoured and looking so happy all
the evening, too. She tried hard to bring her mind back to
the matter in hand — something very important, she
knew, to do with her approaching marriage (and certainly
that was important enough). Of course Euphemia knew
roughly what a Marriage Settlement was, but at a certain
point Grandpapa's Will kept coming into it, and all that
part she just couldn't follow at all.

No wonder if she had been thinking of other things for
a few minutes and, some of the time, not even thinking at
all; just looking. How agreeable everything looked! Papa's
cravat, and the way the candle-light shone on the red
plush table-cloth and winked back at her from the little
Attorney's glass of port. And the Attorney himself! *Dear*
little man, with his little tight trousers; and not half as dry
as he liked to appear, either! In a few minutes, when all
this silliness was over, they would all be back in the
drawing-room and she would be sitting at the walnut-
wood grand piano playing 'Sparkling Cascades',[1] while

---

[1] A novelty solo for piano, "Sparkling Cascades (Mazurka brilliante)"
was written c. 1890 by composer and music publisher Langton Williams
(c. 1832–1896).

Adolphus stood beside her, adoring and turning over the pages of the music — always at the wrong places, unless she remembered at the end of the last line but one to give him the imperious little nod which he would tease her about afterwards. How handsome he looked standing behind the Attorney's chair! How respectful he was to Papa! And what fine manly things Dundreary whiskers were! How anybody ... no, but really, she *must* listen, or Papa would be cross again and spoil everything. Oh dear, how difficult it was! They had got on to Grandpapa's Will again. Was it about *her*? Something about "the first and every other son of her body". Oh, why *must* lawyers say such things? And she made a real effort to banish from her fancy the fleeting vision of a long row of tiny little Adolphuses, all the same size, and each equipped with a minute set of Dundreary whiskers, which went dancing through it as she bent her pretty head over the paragraph at which the little Attorney was now pointed with a wrinkled finger ....

"My dear Sir," said the little Attorney, deftly killing two birds, a friendly one and a professional one, with a single stone, "the question now is, whether *you* are attending!"

Sir William Oakeshott-Meering give a slight start, smiled apologetically and nodded his forgiveness of the Attorney's arch rebuke. It was true that his mind had been wandering, and true that he had just spoken too harshly to his daughter for the same offence. But how *suddenly* the clauses of that Will had taken his memory back! It did not seem like remembering — more as if someone had performed an operation on his mind, cutting away with one clean sweep of the knife everything it had accumulated and become since the year 1851. The very atmosphere of that spring afternoon, the very self he had then been, with all those different hopes and expectations, seemed to have come to life again, as if the fourteen years' interval had never been. What a day it was! And what spirits the old man had been in as he signed the Will it had taken Lushington so long to prepare! They had both chaffed Lushington mercilessly (and not without sly allusions to his charges) about its length and the number of remote possibilities he had provided for. He had been instructed to keep the estates in the male line for ever, or at any rate as long as the law made it possible, and, like all lawyers, he had used a long string of jargon, quite half of which, if it meant anything at all, appeared to mean exactly the opposite. After polishing off all little Charlie's male issue and all his unborn younger brothers, he had started all over again on Euphemia and *her* issue, making the same dry response — "Just in case, you know" — to all their pretended expostulations. And in the middle of it all the door had burst open, and little Charlie, who had somehow got loose from his nurse, had come romping in with a great shout of laughter, with Euphemia, just three years old, running after him, but pausing, in the manner of little girls, awestruck on the threshold at the sight of her Grandpa and a strange gentleman both at the same time. They had broken off business for five minutes to introduce the children to Lushington, who had taken Euphemia on his knee and let her play with his watch-chain and seals, while they all looked on at Charlie's antics. Sir William and his father both saw, and each knew that the other saw, so much more than a little curly-haired boy of seven passing in and out of the sunshine that streamed in through the library window. They did not love him any the less as a child because he was also a transparency through which they beheld a long line of Oakeshott-Meerings stretching endlessly away into futurity. It was the long line and the child together that made them feel so happy.

Oh, well — but Euphemia was seventeen now, and on the verge of getting married. Certainly you couldn't expect her to understand a Disentailing Deed and a Marriage Settlement at the same time, but, deuce take it, her father had thought, as the wave of bitterness and resentment swept over him, she was old enough to attend and try …

"Are you attending?" said Burden in a sharp, disagreeable voice. The Abstract of Title had been much too long to try and examine in the Office, so we had brought it home with us, and were now sitting in front of the fire reading it together. We had gone once hurriedly through it from beginning to end, and now Burden had begun again at the end and was working backwards, beginning with the Vendor, going on through the speculative builder, the two Estate Development Companies and the astute gentleman who had bought a parcel of acres for £2,000 in October 1936 and sold them for £8,000 in the following May, and hoping to reach a point somewhere among the Trustees behind which it would not be necessary to go.

"Eh?" I said. "What's that? Of course! What did you say?"

"I said I couldn't see why they couldn't have started with the Marriage Settlement. Even that goes back to 1865. I really do think you might put some work into it, Burgeon. You're supposed to know more about this end of the Abstract than I do!"

I ignored the last part of his remark. "Because," I said quietly and efficiently, "Lady Wrinkworth, or Euphemia Oakeshott-Meering (as she then was), had only an equitable entail to settle."

"Why *equitable*?" asked Burden irritably.

"Because she only had it in remainder expectant on the death of her father," I said, even more quietly and more efficiently.

"Was that William or Thomas?"

"Sir William Oakeshott-Meering, the Tenant-for-life. If you'd been attending yourself just now, you'd have remembered the Disentailing Deed, executed on the same day as the Marriage Settlement, whereby the Settlor, with the consent of the Tenant-for-life (who was of course the Protector of the Settlement) ——"

"All right!" said Burden hurriedly. "We'll go back to the Root."

"—— and by virtue of the Infant Settlements Act and a special Order of the Court of Chancery," I continued inexorably, "barred the entail, turning it into an equitable fee simple, which she then granted to the Trustees of the Settlement made upon her marriage with the Hon. Adolphus Wrinkworth."

While I was rolling all this out with (I confess) a certain relish, Burden had already turned back to the front page

and the Root of Title, being the Will of Thos. Oakeshott-
Meering, Bart., made on the 4th day of April 1851,
whereby he devised (inter alia): –

> ALL THAT His Capital messuage or Mansion House
> called Oakeshott House with the Coachhouse Stables
> Edifices Buildings Gardens Lands and apurtenances
> thereunto belonging situate lying and being in the
> Parish of Oakeshott-cum-Ringwood aforesaid late in
> the occupation of his son William Oakeshott-Meering

> AND ALSO ALL AND SINGULAR his Manors
> Messuages buildings barns stables gardens orchards
> lands tenements and hereditaments situate lying and
> being in the several Parishes or Hamlets of Oakeshott,
> Ashton, Medworthy, Ringwood and Shepherd's
> Yeadon or any or either of them in the County of
> Berkford with their appurtenances

TO HOLD the same

UNTO his Trustees their heirs and assigns for ever TO
THE USE that his said Trustees should stand seised of
the said estates

IN TRUST for his said Son William Oakeshott-Meering
and his assigns during his life

with Remainder

IN TRUST for his Grandson Charles Oakeshott-
Meering and his assigns during his life

with Remainder

IN TRUST for the first and every other son of the body
of his said Grandson Charles Oakeshott-Meering
successively in tail male

with Remainder

IN TRUST for the first and every other son of the body of his same Grandson successively in tail

with Remainder

IN TRUST for the first and every other daughter of the body of his same Grandson successively in tail

with Remainder

IN TRUST for the second and every other son of the body of his said son William Oakeshott-Meering successively in tail

with Remainder

IN TRUST for the first and every other daughter of the body of the said William Oakeshott-Meering sucessively in tail …

"Mm," said Burden, "she seems to come at the bottom of a fairly extensive list. What about all those prior estates?"

"There's a recital in one of the later Deeds to the effect that Sir William Oakeshott-Meering had no further children after Euphemia."

"But what about the *grandson's* entailed interest?"

"Charles?"

"Yes."

"He didn't have any entailed interest."

"Yes, he — Oh no. I see! He only gets a life interest after his father's life-interest. But his *children* all take entailed interests. How do you clear them off!"

"It's all there," I said patiently.

I turned back one at a time the first three of the large brief-size pages, each of which crackled as it went over, shutting our faces from the fire for a moment before it dropped in front of our knees, where it dangled from the fastening on the left-hand top corner; and I pointed to a single line, all by itself at the top of page 6: –

1861 May 9th Charles Oakeshott-Meering died a bachelor aged 17 years or thereabouts

There was a moment's pause.

"Rather a nice title," I said diffidently.

"I call it a perfectly foul one," said Burden. "Not only is it thirty pages long, but there is nothing whatever to show identity. There's no plan on the Will, naturally. There's no plan on the Disentailing Deed or the Marriage Settlement. Then you get one or two plans on odd Deeds of Appointment, showing a lot of fields with a stream running through them, which seem to fit with each other all right. But there is nothing whatever to connect these with the plan on the Purchaser's Contract. The house we're buying might be a hundred miles away, for all we know."

And he began fidgeting with the pages of the Abstract and the interleaved plan-tracings to demonstrate his point.

What was that about 'plans'? said Thos. Oakeshott-Meering very quietly, so that Burden did not hear. *Didn't I make enough? Where are all mine?*

"ARE YOU ATTENDING?" shouted Burden again, as he thrust the plan on the Contract rudely under my nose.

Whereupon I dragged my attention dutifully back to the piece of transparent blue paper, neatly ruled with a row of parallel, straight, numbered strips, one of which was coloured pink to indicate *No. 35 Meering Avenue.*

V

RHEMATOPHOBIA[1]

I HOPE I SHALL never tell any child of mine that "sticks and stones may break his bones but words can never hurt him!" It is a wicked lie; but it is a lie that was told to me in my own childhood more than once, when I required to be fortified against some dreaded interview or other.

Generally speaking, it is the meanings of words and the tone in which they are spoken which are the cause of pain. I have only lately realised that mere words, as such, irrespective of tone or meaning, mere quantity of utterance apart altogether from its quality, can inflict as much pain as a rebuff or a cold reply to an affectionate question. The pain is of the *longus levis* rather than the *gravis brevis* variety[2], but who shall say whether a night of mild but insistent toothache is better or worse than half an hour at the dentist's?

During the seven or eight hours of each day that Burden spends sitting at his desk he rarely sits alone with me for five minutes without the door opening to admit something new. The something new may be a clerk or a client, but whichever it is it will be new in the sense of being an interruption to something else on which he

---

[1] Most likely Barfield's own coinage. His definition is given on p. 38 of this volume: "fear and hatred of the spoken word."

[2] Cicero, *De Finibus* 94–95. In this passage, Cicero is disagreeing with Epicurus on the subject of pain: "*si gravis dolor, brevis ... si longus, levis.*" "If pain is severe, it is brief ... if it is long, it is mild."

has just succeeded in fixing his mind. In addition to this, the telephone bell rings anything between ten and thirty times during the day, always faintly startling, always heralding something new and possibly alarming, always bringing a mental jerk. This is the petty jerk. The grand jerk occurs when two or more petty jerks are combined. For instance, a clerk or client is in the room, talking; while he is there the telephone bell rings and the caller's business is such that it has to be dealt with then and there; while the caller's business is being 'dealt with' (a phrase, by the way, which seems to imply an easy consciousness — generally absent from Burden's mind — of the dealer's adequacy to the situation), the door opens and a note is handed to Burden telling him that XY is on the other line, possibly with a trunk call and almost certainly in an agitated frame of mind. Just as a complicated mathematical formula is a system of brackets within brackets set out in space, so Burden's mental life of attention and concentration is chopped up into a series of interruptions within interruptions extended in time. Day after day after day appears to him in retrospect as a series of frustrated attempts to pick up the broken thread of what was to have been the main business of the day before. All the time spent on that main business has been spent in getting back on to the starting line, no progress whatever has been made and he seems to himself to have wasted the entire day. Like Alice Through the Looking Glass, he is out of breath with running at full speed in order to keep up with himself remaining in the same place.

I am not commiserating him especially. Thousands of people live the same sort of life, and some of them are said to have three or four telephones in their rooms and to be capable of speaking through all of them at the same time, making in the process decisions on which the lives and happiness of hundreds of thousands depend. The world is at war and most of Europe is under German occupation with the firing-squad never out of sight. Relatively speaking, Burden is one of fortune's favourites. My only business is to record the effect which his experiences are having on him and, through him, upon myself. I have already given my reasons for setting myself this small domestic task, and to repeat them here would add nothing to any cogency they may possess.

The most alarming effect is a fear and hatred of the spoken word. This has become chronic in Burden, and of late I have noticed that I am catching it from him. It is not particularly alarming that at the end of a tiring day Burden should inwardly blaspheme every time the telephone bell or the opening door warns him that he is about to be accosted afresh. It *is* rather alarming that he should at last begin to carry the same mood home with him, to feel that all conversation is an effort and an imposition, to demand of any evening when he is not working, that it shall consist of nothing but supper, silence and bed. It is very alarming indeed when *I* find myself beginning to feel the same, when I want to avoid the children, and on a rare week-end holiday with my best friends — as affectionate and entertaining friends as a man could well ask — my principal reaction to their high spirits is a mental *pauca verba*! or prithee peace! At present I could fancy a holiday alone, or as a guest in a Trappist monastery, better than one with the best friend in the world. And I am wondering if this too is to be a chronic affliction.

Fear of the spoken word. The sounds must be words, and they must be addressed to the patient. Burden and I have not yet come to dislike the sound of the human voice as such. That would be *Phonophobia*. The voice of a nurse or mother babbling nonsense to a contented infant holds no terrors for us, while the relaxed hum of conversation in a crowded saloon-bar is positively remedial. Moreover, the words must be spoken aloud. The most abstruse argument in writing or print, provided we can follow it at our own pace and without fear of interruption, is no irritant. To *Logophobia*, if there be such a complaint, we are immune. The reaction is brought on solely by contact with that collocation of spoken syllables, having a notional reference not immediately apparent from the sounds, which is designated in Greek by the term ῥῆμα and in English by 'word'. If the words are addressed to a fourth party, so that our own intelligence is free to participate or not as it chooses, then *secundum nos*[3] they are not words but sounds, and we remain at ease. The moment of pain is the effort required to convert sound into meaning and to unite that meaning, necessarily anecdotal on its first appearance in the mind, with the meanings of the preceding words and of those which are to follow. This process is normally unconscious, but when the understanding ceases to perform it automatically, it becomes conscious and, in the same

[3] According to us.

moment, painful. It is, too, a feature of the spasm that the self-consciousness of both of us is morbidly intensified, so that there is a close connection between rhematophobia and that other complaint (a mild or incipient form, presumably, of schizophrenia) by which this diary was first begotten, and which it is seeking to remedy.

*   *   *   *   *

It was the latter part of the afternoon of the last day of a crowded week. She was letting a furnished bungalow for three weeks, and she came to see Burden about the tenancy agreement. I feared we were in for a bad time from the moment she began fumbling in her handbag for the letter from the prospective tenant. Any woman may fumble in her handbag, but there is a *way* of doing it, difficult to describe but all too easy to recognise, which betokens a hopeless incoherence of mental process.

Three-quarters of an hour later Burden was still making desperate attempts to obtain, without discourtesy, any one piece of definite information as to this client's desires or intention. Without discourtesy and, if possible, without asking abrupt questions. For an abrupt question (and where there are no natural pauses, every question is abrupt) invariably started her off on an entirely new tack, and meant at least another five minutes lost for ever. Even so there were some questions that were unavoidable. For instance, the lady had a disconcerting habit of substituting the word 'thing' for the crucial noun in her sentence. If this happens once or twice, or only at very rare intervals, and if the reference is the same in each case, it is possible for an agile mind to fill the gap by retrospective guessing. But when it happens frequently, and each time with a different reference, then the game is up. When the word 'thing' means 'electric heater' in one sentence and 'bank account' in the next, there is nothing for it but to say "Thing?" with a smile at once interrogatory and encouraging and take whatever is coming to you.

Somewhere at the back of it all, somewhere — a fitfully looming and dimming shape in that fog of words — there hovered above and about the tenancy agreement, with which it had no connection, an amorphous impulse to obtain Burden's advice about some nuisance which might or might not have been committed by the temporary occupant of the adjoining premises — to be carefully distinguished (by Burden) from the proposed tenant, who had himself occupied them at some time in the past and might still be regarded as responsible for — or at any rate as observing with pleasure — the torts and misfeasances of his successor in occupation. Garbage of sorts kept appearing, it seemed, on the wrong side of the fence. I noticed Burden secretly deliberating whether to ignore this hedgehog altogether, or whether he should make one more forlorn if not positively dangerous attempt to find out if and what she was telling or asking him.

"Did you ever speak to him about it — definitely tax him with it?" he asked, and I saw his heart sink like a stone as she began to expound the history of her relations with the tortious neighbour. She *would* have spoken to him the day before yesterday, or no, it must have been the day before that. (She became intensely interested in fixing, by various landmarks of domestic history, the precise day on which she hadn't spoken and, notwithstanding Burden's earnest assurances that it was of no consequence, took three and a half minutes to do so.) But somehow she hadn't. It was one of those stupid misunderstandings. She had smiled when he asked her about the potatoes which had been wrongly delivered. She had meant to smile exactly as she would have done if anyone else had asked her, but she could see by the way he had looked at her that *he had thought* she was smiling — you know, sort of sarcastically. So she had thought it would be a bad time to say anything. It was so *stupid*. You see ...

All this time one half of poor old Burden's mind was tugging and straining towards a variety of half-remembered things at the back of it — things which he knew *had* to be done during the afternoon that was gliding so steadily away. At last he gave up altogether. We both did. We kept letting the words turn back into pure sound, watching the client's lips move without understanding what she was saying. λόγος[4] slipped gently away and ῥῆμα[5] reverted to bare φωνή[6]. It interposed a little ease, but it brought some bad moments when she paused for a reply.

Fire dissolves, but fire also welds; it operates both to disintegrate and to unite. So it sometimes happens, as on this occasion, that the fiery ordeal which, as I have

[4] λόγος ("logos"). Gk. Lit. "word". This complex term is used here to mean the word, language, as an expression of thought.
[5] ῥῆμα ("rhema"). Gk. A word that is spoken.
[6] φωνή ("phone"). Gk. Sound, voice.
See page 39 for a helpful discussion of these three dimensions of language.

explained, emphasises our separate existence, unites us at the same time in a new understanding and sympathy. When a painful experience is prolonged beyond the point at which it seemed that the strain must become unbearable, the human soul sometimes acquires a sort of tragic second wind. The pain is still there, but it is dulled by a dreamlike awareness of the new and loftier plane on which we are somehow contriving to live. Burden and I both experienced this now, and our relationship seemed to take on a nobler dignity. We exchanged notes, each laying bare to the other his store of sad experience. But not as two wronged and exasperated men; all personal animosity or even irritation was transcended in that larger communion of patient endurance, into which the client too, without her knowing it, seemed to be mysteriously and charitably drawn. At length the silent commerce of our souls clothed itself in a kind of rhythmic, liturgical splendour which, if it could be expressed at all, could only be expressed in verse. At all events, that is the way I have tried to do it: –

IN OMNE VOLUBILIS AEVUM[7]
(OR CLIENT OVER SOLICITOR)

Burgeon: It is all a dream; I am sitting numbed and dead
     And she is holding an enormous hose,
   Pouring a stream of words on my bowed head
     And on and on and on and on it goes.

---

[7] Horace, *Ep.* 1.2.43: "(a river) flows and will flow on, rolling onward forever."

Burden: I think I will go out and buy a shop
            And sell fried fish or furniture or flowers —

Burgeon: Nothing will ever make this woman stop;
            She has been here for hours and hours and hours.

Burden: I will sleep now.

Burgeon: You must not! Rouse, man, rouse!
            A question coming ——we shall need to think!

Burden: She wants my brains to help her let her house;
            Need I know all about the kitchen sink?

Burgeon: Somewhere the post is waiting to be signed —
            Somewhere a hand is crawling round a clock —

Burden: Two hundred things are pressing on my mind: –
            Get on to Counsel ... cash ... Conversion Stock ...

            Where am I? *Which* am I? Who spoke that word?
            The kind old buffer dressed up in my clothes?

Burgeon: Or this more intimate Me, unseen, unheard,
            This frenzied maniac screaming soundless oaths,

            Racked ... venomous ... (Hush! The garrulous are
               the lonely!) —
            Oh little Sister in this vale of woe!
            We hate you not, even love you a little ——only

Both: Go, madam, go! Please go! FOR GOD'S SAKE, GO!

VI

THE THINGS THAT ARE CAESAR'S!

To THOSE WHO have not known him as long as I have, I suppose Ramsden must seem a rather extraordinary sort of chap. His hat, for instance — but it may well be (indeed, there is evidence that it *is*) unnecessary to draw attention to that. For there are other things about him that are extraordinary even to me. Surprising as it may seem to any reader of these sub-acid pages, I am blessed with a number of exceptionally good friends. From all of them I like getting letters; but there is only one whose handwriting on an unopened envelope still gives me the authentic *thrill* of youthful friendship, and that is Ramsden.

Why? It will not be a sufficient answer to this question, but may perhaps throw some light on it, if I mention that in any letter, however brief, from Ramsden I expect to find at least one quotation, philosophical quillet, gibe or cryptic allusion, to the eye of any third party either meaningless or idiotic, but pregnant symbols to us of a period of intellectual intercourse long since woven into the stuff of our lives and taken up into whatever we can claim of wisdom and insight. Perhaps 'wisdom' is too pretentious. A disconcerting feature of these letters is, that parts of them are liable of their own accord to recur to my mind at odd moments later in the day, thereupon contorting my face into a slow, peculiar grin. Burden says it is something about half way between Mona Lisa and the Cheshire Cat. I doubt if this is fair, but must admit that the second comparison is not wholly inapt, because, although my face (as I have explained before) is invisible, the grin, according to him, is not. It is therefore inevitably associated with Burden himself, and has been known to cause him considerable confusion in the street or the railway carriage by eliciting either a haughty stare or an even more alarming acknowledgement from any personable member of the opposite sex who happens to be in the way when it arrives.

The particular letter which I have in mind, however, was one which disappointed these savoury anticipations. It was lying on our table when we reached the Office one morning a few months ago, and I opened it, only to be reminded with a jerk that Ramsden is a client as well as a friend. I swallowed my disappointment and handed the letter to Burden, who scowled at it.

"Is it anything urgent?" he snapped.

"Not particularly."

"Well, bring it up again this evening, will you? I haven't started on the day's ordinary post yet, let alone any new stuff. Yes? Hulloa!" he cried, picking up the telephone, which rang at that moment. "Hulloa! HUL-LOA!" he yelled into the insulting silence which the instrument continued to maintain now that it had fulfilled its principal function of making him jump.

I decided to bring the matter up later on.

It is necessary to explain that Ramsden is a man of letters. He writes, not for a living (the income by which he normally supports himself being assessed under

Schedule E)[1] nor for reputation, but because he can't help it. During the first twenty years of our acquaintance the writings of Ramsden remained, like my own, a purely and decently literary phenomenon, but two or three years ago one of his books (not by any means the one I should have chosen) began for some incomprehensible reason to sell to the general public. It was followed quickly by another, the first impression of which disappeared from the stocks like a plate of buttered scones. And of course shortly after this the royalties began to flow in — or would have done.

This was the point I had most difficulty in explaining to Burden that evening. "You see," I said, "he's never had the money at all."

"Why not?"

"He just gives it away."

"What's he want to do that for?"

"Well, that's *his* business, surely."

"Well, if he gave it away, he must have had it."

"No. He just writes to his publisher and says 'Send a cheque for £50 to John Doe' or 'Pay the next lot to the Home for Retired Professors of Ichthyosophy' and so on."

"Ah," said Burden: "which was it, *alienation* or *application*? We must see those letters."

"He hasn't kept copies."

"No, he wouldn't."

---

[1] Schedule E is the section of England's Inland Revenue tax code which covers income from employment and offices.

"And now he's got this account from his publisher showing another £2,003 due to him and a letter along with it advising him, before they start sending it all over the place on his instructions, to think about income tax a bit."

Burden whistled. I saw he was getting interested: "How much has he given away already?"

"About £1,500."

"Has he paid any income tax on it? By Jove! has he *ever* paid *any* tax on *any* royalties?"

"I imagine not. But he doesn't seem so much concerned about that. He writes us because someone has told him he 'ought to sign some sort of deed'."

"Poor fish!" said Burden kindly. "What is his total income from all sources?"

"I don't know. We can find out from the Bank."

"We must do so. Meanwhile tell him he had better do nothing. It's generally safe to tell clients to do nothing for a bit. Above all, tell him to hang on to that money."

After that Burden took a keen personal interest in the matter. He investigated the exact circumstances in which the royalties had been disposed of, and came carefully to the conclusion that the income had not been alienated before it was due, and must therefore 'attract' (to use the affectionate expression favoured by Inland Revenue officials) income tax. He got full particulars of Ramsden's income from the Bank and perused them like mad. He began doing calculations on the backs of envelopes in the train. He used to see the figure £2,003 written in letters of fire across the ceiling of his bedroom after he put the light out. Finally he took an accountant in and, after the accountant had had it for a weekend, he telephoned to Burden. Burden began to chuckle delightedly.

"What is it?" I asked, as he rang off.

"We have just agreed that the whole of the £2,003, after paying income tax and surtax on itself, will be used up in paying income tax and surtax on the royalties Ramsden has already given away. It should come out almost exactly right. A pure coincidence, of course, but rather neat! By the way, if he *had* done what he meant to, and given this lot away too, the whole of his ordinary salary for the next two years would have gone in paying arrears of tax on the royalties he had never had. If the royalties had fallen off at the same time, he would probably have gone bankrupt! Ha! ha!"

"Ha! ha!"

Burden and I went into consultation, and it was eventually decided that I should see Ramsden, endeavour to explain this to him, and then have a long talk with him about his future course of action. I was to advise him to appoint Burden his charitable trustee, to whom he would then covenant to pay all or most of his future royalty income. This would be paid under deduction of tax, and Burden would annually recover the deducted tax from the Inland Revenue and hold it available for further similar adventures in the art of alleviating other people's misfortunes.

Now, there is a peculiar difficulty we have always had in advising Ramsden: I mean, I am *not invisible* to him. This caused us a lot of trouble at first and a lot of embarrassment and confusion, but eventually we got round the difficulty by arranging that he should never see *Burden* at all. All interviewing is done by me, therefore, though Burden still occasionally writes the letters. I managed to combine this one with an ordinary friendly visit. As I approached the subject, I had the usual strange mixture of feelings. I found myself wondering anxiously what Burden would have said if he had been doing it — at the very moment when I was also telling him to get behind me. I felt nervous, at ease, glad, sorry, irritated, amused all at the same time. The client you have started trying to get rid of from the moment he began to talk is a common enough phenomenon and is, of course, very exhausting. The client who starts trying to get rid of *you* (or at all events of the business you have with him) at an equally early stage in the proceedings is comparatively rare. I know only one instance. And though it certainly cannot be called exhausting, it is rather disconcerting. The 'long talk' lasted about three minutes.

"Well, what did you decide?" asked Burden next day.

"Leaves it entirely to me," I said importantly. "Doesn't even want to understand."

"Probably can't," said Burden. "The artistic temperament."

I had been waiting for this — waiting for it ever since I heard him talking about Ramsden on the telephone. I thought of the greasy journalist's mixture, compounded of greenery-yallery, muddle-headedness, drift and adultery, which did duty for an idea in Burden's mind when he used this cliché. And I thought — well, I thought of Ramsden, with his morale in the skies and his mind blowing steadily out of them, a strong wind edged like a razor. And then I let fly: –

"If you pretend to think, you — you *parrot*," I said between my teeth — "that Ramsden doesn't understand this twaddling muck, because he is incapable of it — is that what you say? Is it? Is it? *Is* it?" I had taken him by the shoulders and was shaking him viciously. But I stopped when I saw the strange effect it had on him.

"Oh, I'm *sorry!*" he said sullenly, straightening his tie: "I forgot I was talking to you. I took that line with the chap at the Bank, and it was just right — made him get all helpful." He turned his head away and went mumbling and grumbling on to himself: "One line to this person — another line to that — give up *having* any opinions of me own altogether — begin to wonder if I exist at all soon!" And to my amazement I heard him give a loud sniff.

I laid my hand on his shoulder, but gently this time. "Why, good gracious me," I said. "If that man liked — er, if he *had* liked ..." I tailed off rather weakly.

Burden seized this advantage to say in a choky voice: "Well, you told me yourself he *didn't* understand."

"I said he didn't *want* to. Man alive! can't you *see*? He doesn't understand on purpose — to save himself the trouble — to keep his mind clean. He — oh *gosh!*" I moaned. "If *only* I had done the same!"

Then Burden said mournfully: "Anyway, I know these clients who leave the whole thing to us and ask no questions. It'll probably come back on you."

"How do you mean, 'come back'?" I asked.

"You'll see, I expect."

After that Burden proceeded to draft a Deed of Covenant, by which Ramsden covenanted to pay over to him any royalties he received for some time into the future, and a neat little Trust Deed, by which he (Burden) declared that he would hold any money he got from Ramsden under the Deed of Covenant on trust, firstly, to pay the costs of the neat little Trust Deed and, secondly, to apply it to such charitable purposes as Ramsden might from time to time direct. Then he made complicated arrangements with Ramsden's Bank to ensure that he got the right amount paid to him after deducting the right amount of tax. Then he opened an account of his own and procured a little charitable cheque-book and asked Ramsden for his instructions, and felt very benevolent as he wrote out the cheques and sent them off with gracious letters.

I pass over Ramsden's real or simulated attempts to understand this part of the business. They are unworthy of the man. Suffice it to say that there was a period during which he was liable, if not watched, to send anybody — Burden, his Bank, or the Inland Revenue — a cheque for any amount, together with an incomprehensible letter saying how it was made up. Soon, however, he got what he had wanted all along, which was a letter from me saying he was not to bother about all this, but simply to ask from time to time how much money there was in the Trust account.

Things seemed to be going pretty well. But I noticed that Burden was going about with a worried look. I asked him what was the matter, and he told me. It had been all right so far, he pointed out, but no actual claim for

repayment of income tax (and that was the point of the
whole thing) could be made until after April 5th, about
nine months ahead. Suppose, when that time came, the
Inland Revenue refused to accept the Deed of Covenant
and the neat little Trust Deed as effective! *Then* where
should we be?

Well, Solicitors' lives are largely made up of these
worries, and they are not the less harrowing at the time
because in the end they generally clear themselves up —
as this one did. For Burden found a kind section in one of
the Finance Acts, which seemed to suggest that Deeds of
this sort could be submitted for approval at any time,
without waiting till a claim could be made. So he
submitted them for approval, and they were approved
without a murmur, and peace and an atmosphere of
subdued triumph reigned in the house of Burden and
Burgeon, but a triumph which, alas, I knew it would be
hopeless to try and share with Ramsden.

Meanwhile Burden had also been engaged in tactfully
disclosing to a suspicious Inspector of Taxes the fact that
his client had earned several thousands of pounds in the
last year or two which he had not thought it necessary to
include in his income tax returns. He went into every
detail himself, and at last the assessments were agreed
and the Collector's demands came in. And lo! the
coincidence had come to pass as predicted. £2,003 almost
to a half-penny!

Here was another triumph for Burden, who makes no
claim to expertise in the accountancy side of income-tax
work. And now the time was come, and I arranged to

meet Ramsden for dinner one night, with full details ready in my waistcoat pocket, and get a cheque from him to cover the unpaid tax.

Next morning Burden asked me if I had got it. Yes, I said, I had got it all right.

"Show him the figures?"

"He didn't want to see the figures."

"Say anything?"

"Well, yes. He asked me if it was usual, when a man got £2,003 income, to have to pay £2,003 tax on it."

"I told you it would come back," said Burden.

We looked at one another.

"Come, Burden!" I said genially, clapping him on the back (for I was in good spirits that morning). "Confess this is the pleasantest job you have done since you started to practise."

He confessed.

"Your hand on it?"

He smiled, in a pawky little way which became him rather well, and held out his hand.

I seized that hand. I placed it behind my waist. I waltzed an unresisting partner gravely round and round the Office! Yes, there is no doubt about it, Ramsden *is* an extraordinary sort of chap. Personally ... but that would take us much too far.

VII
CESTUIS QUE TRUSTENT[1]

SOMETIMES BURDEN AND I get on famously together. When there is not much business coming in, very little pressure, no strain, no grand or petty jerks, I occasionally find myself admiring his professional manner (just like a *real* solicitor!), his 'probity' and the general atmosphere of ripe benevolence which he seems to me, during these illusory and brief interludes, to diffuse about him. Occasionally I tell him about it. He purrs! "Depend upon it, you're right, Burgeon!" he says: "Why, look how I am dealing with this very client now — easy, affable, confident — exactly the thing! And this is only one example. I am not only confident; I *inspire* confidence! That's not all. Think of the wide and varied circle of clients in all walks of life, relations of all ages and sizes, company directors, ladies, little jobbing builders, workmen, young men about town, soldiers, nurses, literary men, all reposing their affairs in *my* hands, all trusting *me*, consulting *me* — and most of 'em, obviously pleased to see me when they come in! What?"

I nod approvingly: "And for some inscrutable reason never quite guessing what a hopelessly flustered and palpitating chump you really are!" I add.

---

[1] Legal term (Anglo–French). Those who will benefit from a trust.

He laughs and then it may happen that a fit of almost maudlin candour comes over him. "As a matter of fact," he says, lowering his voice, "when it comes to winning the confidence of clients, I rely a good deal on you, old chap! They don't see you, but they like to feel you're about in the room somewhere!"

I am afraid that's true. I am a sort of pandar.

Curiously enough, these affable phases of ours are associated in my mind more especially with the equity side of the practice. Anything to do with a settlement or trust — especially if Burden himself is one of the trustees — seems to put us on particularly good terms with one another. This morning, for instance, when he had to interview the tenant-for-life under the Cattermole Settlement: the morning's post was largely disposed of; Burden's table was clear and tidy; and yet it was still reasonably early in the day. The telephone bell rang, the tenant-for-life was announced, and Burden sent for the deeds with considerable complacency. He had had a good look at them at home during the weekend, so he could expect the rare additional comfort of knowing what he was talking about. He untied the red tape and rang through to the outer office, telling them to show the tenant-for-life in.

When the door opened, it admitted not only the tenant-for-life — young, rather good-looking and what interested me (of course) much more, rather *good*-looking — but also along with her the remainderman. Burden had heard rumours already that the remainderman's father was not all he should be. A bit of a scaramouch, in fact. Fortunately the scaramouch had no interest at all under the Settlement, couldn't touch a penny of the capital, or the income either. The tenant-for-life now proceeded to confirm these rumours and to enquire whether she could obtain any of the trust capital to assist herself and the remainderman in the difficult business of living. Burden reassured her on the point and initiated her gently into the mysteries of 'hotchpot'. I noticed that he enjoyed doing so almost as much as if he were bestowing a personal gift on her! Presently she went on to speak of more general problems of domestic economy, and in these also Burden showed her that he could take a fatherly interest. He sympathised over the absence of domestic servants and the endless washing-up. She had had to bring the remainderman with her because there was no one else at home except a rather supine relative, in whose care she was not disposed to leave him for more than an hour or so at a time. And so on. Burden didn't seem as restless as usual and, as there was nothing particular for me to do, I gradually became interested in the back of the remainderman's neck.

I found the place at which his hair came to an end extremely attractive, and I felt I ought to draw Burden's attention to it.

Burgeon (quietly): Look!

Burden: I know!

Burgeon: Why is that particular spot always so enchanting?

Burden: I don't know. Has it something to do with the angle at which the head is bent, the attitude of absorbed attention?

Burgeon: 'Thou best philosopher ...' But look at the *skin*! How could there ever be so much delicacy and so much dignity combined?

> Δός μοι πρός θεῶν
> μαλάκοῦ χρώτος ψαῦσαι τέκνων ...[2]

Burden (savagely): Shut *up*, you ass!

I knew at once what had happened. It wasn't the first time. Talking to me Burden hadn't heard a single word of what the tenant-for-life had been saying for the last thirty seconds. He now had the difficult job of filling in the gap *ex post facto*[3] without giving the game away. Burden is well practised in this awkward and anxious art, but on the present occasion I quickly saw that he was getting into deep water, as the tenant-for-life had chosen that particular thirty seconds to introduce an entirely new topic. The poor chap simply had not the faintest idea what she was talking about. He might at any moment have committed himself to a really startling ineptitude, if I had not come to the rescue with a suggestion. I whispered it to him:

Burden: It's risky, you know!

Burgeon: Never mind. Take my tip. Try it?

Burden (dubiously): All right!

---

[2] Euripides, *Medea* 1402–3. "By the gods, allow me to touch the children's delicate skin!" It appears that Burgeon is disregarding the context of this quotation, for this is Jason, fruitlessly begging Medea to allow him to embrace the bodies of his murdered children.

[3] Legal Latin. Lit. "after the deed." Retroactively.

He looked up at the tenant-for-life with the most disarming smile I could manage for him: "Do you know," he said boldly, "I'm frightfully sorry, but I was so fascinated by the back of your baby's neck that I missed a good deal of what you were saying just now. I'm afraid you'll have to forgive me as best you can and repeat yourself!"

As a matter of fact, I meant him to word this apology *much* more charmingly. It was to have been a humble supplication for mercy, and he was to have addressed her as 'dear lady' or even possibly 'good madonna'. (This sort of thing, by the way, can still be done occasionally; they understand very well when the intention isn't quite all *per jocum*[4] — and rather like it.) But Burden said he absolutely drew the line at that, said she didn't come from that kind of home.

Anyway, it worked beautifully. She looked down at the remainderman with a smile and up at Burden with another and then went back over it all again. I heard the old boy panting faintly with relief and congratulating himself. From a client-holding point of view, he told me afterwards, it was better than if it had never happened at all. I do hate that man sometimes. Sometimes! Do I ever like him? Well, that raises a rather curious point, which I might as well mention here as anywhere else. Sometimes, when he leans back in his chair, more or less at ease, more or less master of the situation for the moment, I see, indeed I feel, something which a good many of our older

[4] For a laugh.

clients have also seen and remarked on. I mean his growing resemblance to our erstwhile senior partner, the late Lifelong Burden. Heredity is a very mysterious thing and, when coupled with love, a very moving one. The love is of the spirit, but the hereditary communion co-existing with it is at once shallower and deeper, because, in creatures as imperfect as Burden and myself, it has a solidity, a *thing-hood* about it, to which the love has not yet attained. It operates in the region between soul and body, the $\psi v \chi \acute{\eta}$ $\theta \rho \epsilon \pi \tau \iota \kappa \acute{\eta}$[5] — nutritive or life-bearing soul — of Aristotelian psychology, the etheric body, as it is best called to-day. Now Burden and I have only one of these between us; so that I can speak of both feeling and seeing this sort of thing. The verb 'to resemble' is transitive, but it is not generally thought of as a verb active. Yet at the times I am speaking of I not only catch glimpses of the resemblance between Burden (in his best moments) and his father, but I half experience the act of resembling, as if it were my act. To some extent, in his adoption of some little gesture or attitude or expression, it sometimes really is my act, a deliberate one too; inasmuch as the muscular impulse is consciously felt before it issues in movement and is purposely left unchecked. The instant after, I see the effect from outside, and it is in these instants that I do occasionally feel something approaching to affection for that animated rag-bag of doubts and worries, my partner Burden. In the same moment I silently salute Lifelong, where he is now, and

[5] Aristotle, *De Anima* 413a28.

pray that the Gods are bestowing on him *ex gratia* that fullness of confidence in himself which he inspired so easily in others, while he was here, without the comfort of sharing it with them.

But all this is a quite unforeseen digression from the trusts of the Cattermole Settlement. Needless to say we had the usual discussion during the day. Burden began it by nudging me with his elbow in the peculiarly irritating way he has and saying:

"Well, nothing wrong this time, Old Boy!"

Burgeon: "What do you mean?"

Burden: "I mean the jolly old profession is functioning. Justly and beneficently. If ever two human beings are entitled to help and protection, that woman and her baby are. She couldn't do without a solicitor and" (tapping himself on the chest) "here he is!"

Burgeon: "Yes. Your foul contentment has nothing whatever to do with the beneficence of the law. It's simply because there's a nice bit of trust work with nothing contentious in it, no time running and a good fat fund to get the costs out of, so that the client won't feel it in her own pocket!"

Burden: "Oh, come now! That's not quite fair! There's no reason why I shouldn't enjoy getting properly paid. I do a good deal of work without it, you know! The other's true too. Why, you once told me yourself that you liked the flavour of equity!"

Burgeon (gloomily): "Yes, but it's all based on property. If that baby hadn't got an interest in some money, he could go to perdition for all the law cares!"

Burden: "Well, I don't care. The principle's right. It's got to start somewhere. I remember your pointing out, when we were reading Snell's *Equity* for the Solicitor's Final, that many of our words for moral qualities, like *gentle*, *noble* and so forth, were originally words for class distinctions that had a good deal to do with property. So much the better for property, you said. Once you have created a principle, you can spread it. Equity *has* spread. What about the Guardianship of Infants Acts? You don't need any property, if you go under them."

Burgeon: "You've got to have enough money to pay the costs!"

Burden: "Now you're hedging!"

Burgeon: "Oh well, anyway, the reason why you're so jolly pleased with yourself is just that you're going to have an easy time and have been getting on rather well with a nicely-dressed lady client. *I* saw you!"

Burden (indignantly): "I *like* that! What about you! You and your 'good madonnas'!"

Burgeon (with dignity): "It was the remainderman I was really interested in. The tenant-for-life was purely ancillary."

Burden: "Oh, you think too much! They made a very pretty picture together, and you know it as well as I do."

Burgeon (thoughtfully):

> "Ich sehe dich in tausend Bildern,
>   Maria, lieblich ausgedrückt,
> Doch keins von allen kann dich schildern
>   Wie meine Seele dich erblickt.

Ich weisz nur dass der Welt Getümmel
Seit dem mir wie ein Traum verweht
Und ein unnennbar süsser Himmel
Mir ewig im Gemute steht!"[6]

We were just arriving back from lunch, and the last line of my quotation from Novalis was interrupted by the telephone bell, which rang out as we entered the room. Burden strode savagely to the instrument, and became at once involved in conversation with an old and valued client who had rung up to explain that the water from the lavatory in the flat above was coming through into his flat and what was he to do about it. While he was talking Burden read a little note which the office-boy had left on his table, requesting him to ring up the tenant-for-life as soon as he came in. As a general rule this sort of thing frightens him, but there *couldn't* be anything wrong here. It would be just some trifle she had forgotten to ask him during the morning. He got rid of the old and valued client and, without trepidation, through to the tenant-for-life.

There was a whole lot wrong.

The tenant-for-life had had to go out for an hour after she got back, leaving the remainderman in charge of the

---

[6] *Mary, I see you tenderly depicted*
in a thousand pictures,
But none of them can express
The way my soul regards you.

I only know that since then,
the world's clamor passes by me like a dream,
and an indescribable sweet heaven
is always in my spirit.
    "Marienlied" by Friedrich von Hardenburg (Novalis).

supine relative. While she was out, the scaramouch had gone to the house, got round the supine relative and kidnapped the remainderman, leaving a note to say he was taking him to his mother's house, where the child would be well looked after. (Burden groaned.) Wasn't this a *crime*? asked the tenant-for-life. Burden groaned again as he tried to explain to her that without an Order of the Court the father had just as much right to the custody of the infant as she had — perhaps more.

Two things contributed in about equal proportions to disturb Burden's peace of mind during this conversation. The first was a new note which began to creep into the tenant-for-life's voice. It was a note of bewildered and even indignant contempt for the incompetence and obtuseness of 'the law', a term of which the extension was clearly wide enough to take in personnel, including her own legal adviser. The second was the ineluctable fact that the situation was one which called for prompt action, and that he had not the faintest idea what that action ought to be. With the beginnings of perspiration gathering on his brow, he made tentative and rather shamefaced enquiries as to the possibilities of self-help by way of counter-kidnap, and learned with relief that they could be ruled out. Finally he advised her that the best course was an application to the Court, without specifying too precisely at the moment what she would be applying for or to whom. She said she would like to come along and see him straight away. Consternation! And out of it a cheery, confident, almost hand-patting voice that sounds like Burden's crying: "Rather! I shall be in all the afternoon!"

As soon as she got off the telephone, however, the problem began to look fairly straightforward. The remainderman's interest under the Settlement made it easy enough to get him into Chancery, and there would be an Originating Summons, no a Writ, no an Originating Summons, issued by the tenant-for-life asking for the custody of the infant. Having regard to the infant's age, the Applicant, being his undoubted mother, was almost certain to succeed, and there would be full solicitor-and-client costs out of the Fund. Apart from the fact that half-a-dozen or more other urgent matters, which he had been wondering, even before the telephone call, how to squeeze into the day, had to be scrambled, scrapped, scraped, skipped, scamped, burked and gerrymandered to make room for the tenant-for-life's call, life looked as if it might become bearable again, after all.

But gone, gone was all that bowery prospect of calm and sunny days. Burden took a hurried and furtive survey of his immediate future, and perceived at least two days of misery, with probably half a night thrown in. I shared his vision and girded my loins. We should be working against time and there would be affidavits. Affidavits!

Well, the first turned out easier than we expected. We simply said we were the infant's mother, and respectfully submitted to this honourable Court that it was for his benefit that we and no one else should be looking after him. Drafted, engrossed, sworn, filed and copy to the scaramouch's solicitor (a beast with an irritatingly experienced and patronising voice, who had come on the scenes shortly after the Summons was served). But then, after about a week, Burden received a copy of the scaramouch's affidavit in reply. Rather well drawn, aggressive and alleging all sorts of surprising and unpleasant reasons why it would be bad for the remainderman to be handed back to the tenant-for-life, supported by two or three affidavits of other deponents — including one by the supine relative, who had had a furious row with the tenant-for-life and gone off in a huff. Most of the allegations sounded pretty fantastic, but they were put convincingly enough to require very careful answering. At least Burden thought so. He wasn't sure. He never is sure.

Up comes the tenant-for-life to the Office again: –

Attending you on your calling going through Respondent's affidavit in detail and taking very full instructions for affidavit in reply thereto, engaged over 3 hours at the end of which you were in tears and we had given up the idea of lunch.

We took the papers home with us and sat up till 4 a.m. The worst of an affidavit is that it does matter how it is worded. Style really does tell. The consequence is that Burden and I have to collaborate over them, quarrelling all the time. He tells me that I am taking much too much time and trouble and that he knows solicitors — meets them in the train every day, old boy — who dictate their affidavits straight off and then go home and play bridge. I bite his head off and tell him to get on with it by himself, then. He smiles in a superior way and refers to the Partnership Agreement. Then we do a bit more work. He cuts out or alters something I want to put in, because it sounds too literary. I contest it at first, but in the end have to agree that in the context his emendation is the better style. Then I bite his head off again for expecting me to lend my vast creative powers to the task of helping him run his horrid little squabbles. Then we both look at the clock and swear at each other and everything in reach and go on to the next paragraph or out into the kitchen to make another cup of tea.

I will say this, though, that when the thing is engrossed and ready for swearing, it looks good. And it *is* good. I back our affidavits against those of any firm I have come against. And they tell, too! I have seen it over and over again. So they ought to! says Burden grudgingly, with about seventy-five per cent more work in them that he can charge for.

This time, just as we were sitting down to the job at 10 p.m. I got rather a nice one in on Burden.

"What are you grousing about?" I said.

"How long are we going to take this time?" he growled. "If we don't get to bed before one o'clock we shall be tired and leg-trembly all the rest of the week!"

"Burden," I said solemnly, "if ever two human beings were entitled to help and protection, that woman and her baby are. She couldn't do without a solicitor and" (tapping him on the chest) "there he is!"

He looked as if he would like to murder me. But he hadn't a word to say.

Wan, blear-eyed and trembly about the legs, Burden and I managed somehow to struggle up to the Office at the usual time next morning, and he lost no time in handing out the scribbled, deleted, interleaved, arrow-and-balloon-ridden mess which he had endorsed *Rough Draft Affidavit of Applicant* — for engrossment. It looked something like the facsimile MS. of *Lycidas*. Later in the morning the engrossment was brought in, and we settled down to our one little titbit of pleasure — looking upon our work and seeing that it was good. And good it was, too. We had just got to paragraph 7 — the one we had quarrelled hardest over — when the telephone bell rang and the tenant-for-life was announced. Come by appointment, of course, to swear the affidavit!

"Tell her I shall be ready in five minutes," said Burden.

We finished reading over the affidavit, and enjoyed ourselves for a moment imagining the uneasiness that would reign in the breast of the scaramouch's solicitor when he got his copy next morning. Then Burden rang the bell.

Steps along the passage. The door opens, and in comes the tenant-for-life — followed by the scaramouch, in the uniform of the Tank Corps, with the remainderman seated firmly on his shoulders and wreathing himself all round his head as if his life depended on his success in converting himself into some new kind of turban.

It appeared they had met and made it up about three hours before we had started drafting the affidavit. Burden hastily rang through to the scaramouch's solicitor, as etiquette demanded, and informed him that his client was at the moment in his (Burden's) Office. Had he any objection to the interview proceeding? Burden expected an outburst, at least of surprise, and rather enjoyed

handing out this bombshell, as he thought. Not a bit of it.
He didn't mind, my dear fellow! He had heard all about it
the night before. I could positively see that superior smile
playing about his lips, as he spoke. There would be a
consent Order giving the two of them joint custody, and
the leave of the Court would be asked to withdraw the
affidavits already on the file.

Somehow the three of them looked very nice together,
and I felt distinctly happy. Perhaps I am not damned,
after all. A month or two back I had persuaded Burden to
get in a bottle of sherry and some glasses and hide them
in the safe. He had grumbled, said it was affectation or
antiquarianism, or something on my part, but he had got
them. This seemed to be a fitting occasion, if ever there
was one. So out they came, and the remainderman was
accommodated from the tea-box with a biscuit which
disintegrated steadily during the rest of the proceedings.
I got Burden to try out a jocose allusion to 'the remainder
biscuit', but it didn't work. There was no certain
indication that anybody even heard it.

After they had left, Burden and I looked at each other,
at the affidavit and at the waste-paper basket. Burden
opened his mouth to speak, but I got in first.

"Stop!" I said. "Let it suffice that it was our duty, and
we have done it. Results are irrelevant. Remember what it
says in the *Bhagavad Gita*: –

> Whose works are all free from the moulding of desire, whose
> actions are burned up by the fire of wisdom, him the wise
> have called a Sage.

Having abandoned attachment to the fruit of action, always content, nowhere seeking refuge, he is not doing anything, although doing actions ...

For him there is no interest in things done in this world, nor any in things not done, nor doth any object of his depend on any being.

Therefore, without attachment, constantly perform action which is duty, for, by performing action without attachment, man verily reacheth the Supreme ...

Surrendering all actions to Me, with thy thoughts resting on the supreme Self, from hope and egoism freed, and of mental fever cured, engage in battle ...

Unto the Eternal verily shall he go who in his action meditateth wholly upon the Eternal!

"Anyway," said Burden, "thank goodness there's a nice fat trust-fund behind us to get the costs from!"

And even as he spoke, the icy thought struck him for the first time that perhaps there wasn't. The *status quo ante*[7] had been restored in the home. Could it *really* be said to be for the advancement maintenance or benefit of the infant that Burden's bill should be paid? He hastily rang the bell and gave instructions to start preparing it.

"I must get it delivered and paid before they quarrel again," he said, "while they're still feeling thoroughly pleased with life!"

---

[7] Legal Latin. Lit. The way in which before. Its former state.

VIII
VISION

The Law Society's Hall is not a bad place. You'd think it would be, but somehow it has contrived not to. Once get it clear of those two leprous blights on the urban life of the twentieth century, the typewriter and the telephone, and there is at least a certain restful and, in a limited sense, dignified atmosphere about the profession. Burden and I occasionally lunch there and, if time permits, interpose a little ease in the common room afterwards. There among the solicitors, lulled by the subdued hum of their multitudinous conversations, we take our coffee at a little table from a little tray with a little cup and saucer and a little coffee-pot on it, all specially arranged so that the coffee is a little cold before you actually drink it.

Sometimes we manage to get one of the row of armchairs in front of the fire. We did today. Burden was tired, and he closed his eyes as soon as the coffee was finished. At first the conversations sounded less subdued than when he had had them open. Here and there the uniform murmur turned into distinct voices, and even words, and he became interested for a few minutes in the efforts of a group round one of the little tables not far away to solve the day's crossword puzzle in *The Times*. Very soon, however, the little trickle of dialogue merged again in the general hum, and the hum seemed to grow to a gentle roar, which rose benignantly round Burden's ears like the noise of the sea on a warm summer's day. He became comatose.

In the same measure I myself grew more and more wide awake, and began to look around me at the forms and faces of the circumrecumbent solicitors — among them, by the way, some good friends of Burden's and one or two of my own. It was then that I had my vision of the Absolute Solicitor.

I am at a loss to know how best to convey or in what imagery to furnish forth the true nature of this great *One*, which manifests itself so partially and imperfectly in each of us individual solicitors. It has been said that no-one has ever really seen Tree or Horse, but only trees or horses. Those who would rise in contemplation from the particular manifestation to the underlying Forms of things must train themselves by rising first to intermediate levels. Thus they may learn to perceive, as types, the Deciduous Tree or the Draught Horse. At the other end of creation the interval which yawns between Richard Roe or William Stiles on this side and, on that, Man the seed of Adam, the battleground of warring Principalities and Powers and the raw material of the divine process of redemption, is too great for the perceptive faculty to span at a leap. First we must grasp at intuitions of those intermediate spiritual types which are the realities underlying, not indeed the whole of mankind, but groups of men. They knew this in the Middle Ages with their subtle perceptions of the four 'humours', phlegmatic, sanguine, choleric and melancholic.

The problem is made infinitely more complex by the fact that no one man embodies a single archetype only. They are mixed in us. We distinguish, for example, the melancholic from the choleric man, because in the former the melancholy humour *predominates* over the other three, not because the other three are not also present in his temperament. And it is only by observing a number of such men that we can grope towards an intuition of the quality of melancholy and of the melancholic type in their purity. Nor, when we have done so, can we hope to describe them in that purity. We can only describe some average melancholic man.

In the same way the gulf between, say, Mr. Conrad Cange of Cange, Custody & Co. and the Absolute Solicitor can only be crossed on stepping-stones made of the mediate archetypes: which archetypes are three in number — namely, Lynx, Glossy and Applejohn.

The Lynx is usually a *young* solicitor. That in itself is a misfortune, for youth and solicitoring fadge ill together, as may be seen by observing with attention any group of articled clerks emerging from a lecture or an examination. There is a certain *scrawniness* about the articled clerk, a lack of grace and charm, an indefinable malaise about the way in which his neck emerges from his collar, an alert absence of enthusiasm in his eyes, all of which are unmistakable. Now, the other types of solicitor manage in time to slough off some of these qualities, but the Lynx retains them into the maturity of his powers.

The Lynx has a hungry look about his jaw. His aura is dog-like or wolfish. A wolf is always hungry, and with a craving that is not satisfied even in the moment of devouring. For this very craving is the true life and being of its soul. When it swallows food, there is no accompaniment of savour to the process; hardly even of mastication; there is merely an agonised rush to get outside the thing swallowed. And it is above all in these hurried, joyless motions of swallowing that we perceive the essential nature of the animal. With the human Lynx it is not the physical act of swallowing, but the spiritual one of *over-reaching* that is typical. It is in the moment when he is over-reaching someone that his true nature flashes upon the inward eye of the observer.

The Lynx's proper element is litigation and negotiation. Of course he must do other things as well, but it is in litigation and negotiation that he feels as really at home as his nature permits him to feel anywhere. He is to be found in firms of all sizes and reputations. In the City he acts for pushful companies and their promoters, and the sums about which he litigates and negotiates are substantial in quantity, whether or no they ever existed in cash. In the little streets adjoining the Police Courts and County Courts he acts for anybody who comes along and strives to allay his cravings by getting 6s. 8d. allowed by the Registrar instead of the 3s. 4d. to which he is entitled. At this end of the scale he shades off into a snake type with sloping forehead and shifty eyes. I do not mean (God forbid!) that every solicitor who practises in that environment is of this type. The type (fortunately rare) may appear anywhere, but it reacts to that particular environment in that particular way. At the other end he merges imperceptibly in the Glossy.

Unlike the Glossy and the Applejohn, there is nothing specially characteristic about the room in which the Lynx works. It may be either mean and untidy or dustless, up-to-date and equipped with steel furniture, filing cabinets and bounceable chairs.

You may feel sure of the Lynx's honesty, but never of his sincerity. His soul moves in a realm of advocacy rather than of truth, and it would have been healthier for it if he had been a barrister. For that would have not only afforded greater scope to his bent advocacy, but also taught him to distinguish it from himself. He is fond of beginning his sentences with the words "Quite frankly" because he is never quite frank. He quickly develops the authentic 'poker face'. Underneath the part of his mind that is conversing with you there is always another part working independently, devising, scheming, looking carefully and cautiously ahead. All dealing with him is a strain. You must be perpetually on the look out, or you will wake up next week to find that he has been aiming all along at something you never thought of. There is no professional fraternity between you and him, no common air of mutual candour which you gladly breathe together. And this not (save in very exceptional cases) because he is fundamentally dishonest, but because of the extent to which he inwardly identifies himself with his client. In short, you are never at ease with him.

The Glossy usually wears a black coat and striped trousers. In his youth he prefers a soft black hat to a bowler. His tidy office is well swept and dusted, and may even have some pretensions to taste. It is left clear of papers, which are brought in to him as they are required. The Glossy is better educated than the Lynx and more of a gentleman. He is often to be found occupying such of the better-paid legal appointments in the Civil Service as are open to Solicitors. In private practice he is usually fortunate in his clients, perhaps because he is well-to-do enough to refuse those whom he does not like. Thus, his clients also are usually men or women of some substance. Is it a conveyancing matter he has in hand? Not for him the little speculative builder who comes for building advances, to be drawn stage by stage as the building goes up, and who advertises with a flourish that the purchaser's legal costs are included in the price of the house. *He* is acting for a comfortable family with a small mansion for sale or a company buying up real property on an extensive scale. Is it a probate? You may be sure the estate runs into five figures at least.

He of course acts so as to further his client's interests, but he does not identify himself with them, as the Lynx does. Consequently you may feel quite at ease in negotiation and disagreement with him, even when the clients themselves are embittered.

The Glossy may in theory be of any age. He may remain a Glossy from admission to retirement. Or he may have started his professional life as a Lynx and toned down under the gradual weight of experience. If, however, he has not retired by the age of about 65, one of two things is likely to have happened to him. Either he will be showing marked signs of transition to an Applejohn, or he will have passed into a higher realm altogether; he will be a director of some large company, shipping, insurance or banking; he will be on the Council of the Law Society;

he will be — in short, in one way or another he will have reached those masonic and rotarian altitudes which unobtrusively guide the commercial and professional life of this country in the way they feel it should go.

The true Applejohn, as his name implies, has a face covered all over with little wrinkles, like a stored apple. But this particular one of the Applejohn's characteristics, although it is eponymous, is not absolutely essential. A Commissioner for Oaths, for example, may have a quite ordinary face and yet reveal himself an Applejohn by the very way in which he takes your oath and your half-crown.

The Applejohn is out and out a conveyancing man. He keeps clear of the Courts if he possibly can. The nearest he comes to polemics is his answers to your Requisitions on Title or the alterations in red ink which he inserts neatly on the draft you have submitted for his approval on behalf of his client. Here he sometimes rises to a kind of acid scorn. The best of them, at the end of a long correspondence on some conveyancing point, involving interlocking sub-sections from three or four of the 1925 Statutes, will suddenly floor you with something out of Section 1 or 2 of the Law of Property Act 1925, which nobody else has looked at since he passed his Final. And the experience is invigorating. It is like being suddenly brought back to first principles in a philosophical dispute. But the Applejohn is not so much the philosopher as the craftsman of our profession. I think the little wrinkles have something to do with this. He likes documents as such. He relishes the drafting of them. If he knocks *your* draft about, it is because you have departed in some way from conveyancing practice or precedent, and it grieves his soul. He is an 'Attorney' in the good old sense, carrying an aroma about him of the fast-fading days of parchment and the 'fair and clerkly hand'.

The walls of his room are lined from floor to ceiling with documents and folders. The like also are piled high in profuse disorder on the very large table, or pair of tables, at which he works, and have overflowed on to the floor all round him. He just manages to keep one little space on the table clear enough to write on. No one has ever discovered how he finds what he wants there as quickly as he does — or indeed at all — picking it out of the general hugger-mugger with a thin and often slightly shaky hand.

The Applejohn is never young. He graduated from one of the other types, usually the Glossy. He is for the most part a gentle, kindly soul, easy to get on with in business, but disappointingly dull outside it, unless indeed he happens to have acquired some specialised antiquarian knowledge which it interests you to hear about.

These three humours are to be found mixed in varying proportions in each practising solicitor. When one of the three predominates markedly over *both* the other two, you come nearest to a physical embodiment of the archetype. Then you *almost* see an Applejohn, a Lynx or a Glossy before you in the flesh; and you may properly allude to him as an applejohn (or as the case may be), spelling him without the capital letter. Such temperaments are not exactly rare, but neither are they common. A *single* humour is more likely to be markedly deficient than markedly predominant, and the average solicitor is either a glossy-lynx or a glossy-applejohn (the lynx-applejohn is not found), with the two predominant humours mixed in him in varying proportions.

But the Absolute Solicitor, whom I now perceived in the spirit, stood far beyond and above these faulty approximations. In him none of the three humours was predominant and none deficient, but all three were mingled in just proportion and sweet harmony. The gentleness and sure craftmanship of the Applejohn chimed perfectly with the tact and suavity of the Glossy and, while the latter continued to preserve a balanced detachment from the passions of the client, so as to uphold the fraternity of the profession, the Lynx, tamed now to a trusty bandog, crouched at the feet of both, with a watchful eye open to ensure that the client's true interest should never, never be sacrificed for the sake of gentleness or the love of ease, or to preserve that suavity or that fraternity.

It was an inspiring vision. But in the very moment at which the clouds that had hitherto obscured it melted finally away and it stood before me in sharp outline and crystal purity, Burden stirred in his chair, and I knew that he had pins and needles in the arm on which he had been resting his head. The soothing rumour which had filled his ears turned again into a recognisable hum of human voices in conversation. Now he became aware that some of the voices were more distant, some more near at hand; and now again the little trickle of dialogue behind his chair detached itself from the ocean of sound, and I realised that he realised that the speakers were still engaged on that crossword puzzle. There were four of them, I saw, round the table — two glossy-lynxes, a glossy-applejohn and an applejohn.

"Wordsworth?" we both heard the glossy-applejohn suggest as a tentative solution of the light.

"Who was Wordsworth?" asked the glossy-lynx.

"Wasn't he the fellow who went over to France and seduced some girl?" enquired the other glossy-lynx slowly.

I heard no more.

"Get up!" I said to Burden. "Get back to the Office!" I wanted to be gone now that the vision had faded.

*   *   *   *   *

Whenever I entertain a guest to lunch in the Law Society's Hall, at some point in the proceedings he is pretty sure to ask, with a kind of incredulous awe, if it is really true that practically everyone in sight is a solicitor. As I reply in the affirmative, a faint, politely repressed shudder seems to go through him. He is visibly impressed.

Ought we not, I wondered as we made our way back to the Office today, to take some advantage of the impression that is evidently made on the laity by the unusual sight of a large number of solicitors all gathered together in the same confined space. It may be that we could even combine it with some benefit to the laity itself. We might, for instance, have a porter stationed in Chancery Lane inviting the public in to inspect us and take its choice. Something in the nature of a horse-fair flitted through my fancy. I suppose it is useless to deny that I am sometimes rather light-headed. If the thing became really well-established and traditional, I thought, we might even find ourselves helping to keep alive the vanishing Cries of Old London by adding a new one to them. If so, it ought to have something of the old savour about it. For, after all, it is just the persistent touch of archaism that keeps the profession sweet. How would this do?

> Walk in, ladies! Come and buy, sirs!
> Ripe attorneys! Sound advisers!
> Keep yer profits, cut yer losses!
> Lynxes, applejohns and glossies!
>
> Glossies, applejohns and lynxes!
> Come and pick the one you think is
> Just the one to suit yer fancy!
> Litigations's horrid chancy!
>
> Applejohns with parchment faces!
> Glossies — put 'em through their paces!
> Prime attorneys! Lovely ones!
> Lynxes! Glossies! Applejohns!

IX
CRISIS

THINGS HAVE BEEN getting much worse lately. I feel that some sort of crisis is approaching. What *is* wrong with me? Why, I have been asking myself in the last month or two — why does my inside quiver like a jelly all day? Is it fear? Or what?

At first I wasn't sure whether it was mine or Burden's that was doing the quivering. But Burden said it couldn't be his. He knows the rules and keeps well within them, so he is safe. It is true he has a lot of responsibilities — to his clients, to his staff, to his dependents; to pretty well everyone, it sometimes seems — but there is no reason to suppose that he won't discharge them tolerably well.

He was all right, he said, "It must be yours, old man."

"Mine!" I indignantly replied. "What am I supposed to be afraid of? You know very well I shouldn't turn a hair if the practice went to pot and we were struck off the Rolls to-morrow. In fact I see a lot of advantages in it — for me."

All the same, I am afraid he is right.

Probably the endless procession of troubles and the pressure at which we are working have something to do with it. As to whether this pressure is likely to prove too much for Burden in the end, I don't ever bother to form an opinion. For I do not care a straw whether it does or not. I observe its effects on him with a detached interest and, if I do occasionally speculate how long he can keep it up, I do so simply as a matter of idle curiosity.

But is it going to prove too much for *me*? I sometimes wonder. There is no doubt that somewhere inside something is quivering practically the whole day now. I think it is the expectation of little blows and bruises. *Parva si non fiant quotidie*[1]: the look of the office door when we arrive in the morning; somebody's ill-nature; a snub; a sharp exchange over the telephone; a rumpus over a bill of costs; staff rows (and their name is legion) — tap, tap, tap, you'd think one would get less sensitive, form some kind of protective layer of thicker skin. Not a bit of it. The everlasting succession of taps only serves to keep 'the place' (but what place?) tender and never give it a chance to heal.

Yes, I really begin to feel that a crisis of some sort cannot be avoided. Things are coming to a head.

*   *   *   *   *

When the crisis came yesterday, it began as might have been expected, with one of those interminable, bickering arguments between myself and Burden. As far as I recollect, it went something like this: –

Burden (speaking down the telephone): "Look here, I've been back to my Client, and he says that rather than have all the trouble of further litigation he'll accept your figure

---

[1] *Parva si non fiant quotidie*. Lat. In *The Rambler* (1750), the great English author Samuel Johnson famously quotes this phrase, which appears in *Naturalis Historia* ("Natural History") by the Roman naturalist and philosopher Pliny the Elder (23–79), and translates it as "things which nothing but their frequency makes considerable."

after all … £225 … Yes. In full settlement. Will you write me? Good-bye!"

Burgeon (gently): "That was a lie, you know!"

Burden: "What was?"

Burgeon: "That about your having been back to the Client. It's only half an hour since you told those solicitors that the action must proceed if they wouldn't go to £250. You haven't been near the Client since. He isn't even on the telephone."

Burden: "All right; a conventional lie, then."

Burgeon: "Still, a lie! Moreover, you told them that your instructions would not permit you to settle for less than £250."

Burden (with a nasty ring in his voice): "Did the Client leave it entirely to me or didn't he?"

Burgeon: "He left it to you."

Burden: "To do what?"

Burgeon: "To do the best you could for him."

Burden: "That's equivalent to saying that he would give me any instructions I advised him to give me at any time."

Burgeon: "Is it?"

Burden: "You know it is. Do you seriously suggest I ought to have gone through the motions of first advising him not to let me accept less than £250, and then advising him to change his mind and let me after all. His leaving it to me was equivalent to saying he didn't want the bother of all that. I thought there was just a chance that my telling them I couldn't go below £250 and ringing off would bring them up another £25. Believing that, I should have failed in my duty to the Client if I hadn't acted on it."

Burgeon: "Maybe, but I don't like it much."

Burden (energetically): "Why not? If a client gives me *carte blanche*, that's as much as to say he substitutes me for himself. I represent him *qua* client besides acting for him as solicitor. I am entitled to go to myself for any instructions I like at any moment I like."

Burgeon: "Isn't that casuistry?"

Burden (after a pause): "All right, if you like. Call it that. *Ab abutere ad usum non valet consequentia.*[2] You know what the word 'casuistry' means literally, as well as I do. Better, in fact. It's the science of applying general moral principles to particular cases. If you mean *dishonest* casuistry, I don't agree."

Burgeon: "How do you distinguish the honest from the dishonest?"

Burden: "I suppose, partly by the sincerity of the intention and partly by the validity of the logic with which the application is made."

Burgeon: "What sort of sincere intention justifies lying?"

Burden: "Have you ever told anyone you were glad to see him, when you didn't feel glad at all?"

Burgeon: "Yes, but that was for his sake, neither *for* my own interest nor *against* his."

Burden: "Never mind — was it lying?"

---

[2] Legal Latin. Lit. The results of misuse do not apply to use.

This proverb is usually interpreted to mean that even though a right to do something is often abused, taking advantage of the right does not, in itself, constitute misuse.

Burgeon: "It's different. *You* were deceiving the other side (or trying to — I don't suppose for a moment you succeeded) for the purpose of injuring them."

Burden: "My duty is to help my client. I am paid for it. The matter is contentious, and there is a conflict of interest. I can only help my client's interest by relatively 'injuring', as you say, the other side."

Burgeon: "Certainly you are paid to do it, and may be it's your duty. If you took a job as a slave-driver it would be your duty to drive slaves. But that wouldn't make it any sweeter in the nostrils."

Burden: "This is mere squeamishness. Look. This doesn't happen to be an Employers' Liability case, but it might very well have been. It often has been. *There* the issue is clear enough, surely! You are acting for a workman against a powerful insurance company. He has been badly injured, and needs as badly every penny he can get for himself and his wife and family. A 'man of straw' — with all the resources at the disposal of wealth and education marshalled against him. If he gets nothing, you probably won't charge him more than his out-of-pockets (yes, I know 'Maintenance' and all that: shut up!); but that's by the way. The insurance company puts out feelers for a settlement. He 'leaves it to you, guvnor'. What does he mean by that? He knows that on the other side both the Client and the Solicitor are educated people, clever at bargaining and knowing their ground in advance. On his side, if he tries to take a hand, there will be only one skilled and one unskilled party. Two against one. Do you mean to tell me you are not bound in honour to put him as nearly as possible in the same position as the other side?"

Burgeon: "Um!"

Burden: "What do you mean, 'um'? It'd be a dirty trick to do anything else."

Burgeon: "The choice seems to be between two dirty tricks."

Burden: "Tut! It's like a feint in a duel or a tactical ruse in battle. It's absurd to call it dishonest."

Burgeon: "You partly convince me. Lying and play-acting are a recognised part of bargaining in most countries, I suppose. The vendor in an Oriental bazaar always begins by assuring you that he will be ruined if he accepts a penny less than some figure about 300 per cent higher than he really hopes to get. You decline and say good-morning. He comes down to 250 per cent at the expense of various dependent relatives. You decline again and leave the shop. He runs out after you and calls you back. After about half an hour of this the just price is reached on the footing that his wife and children, who have already spent most of their lives in hospital, are practically certain to die of starvation as the result. You do not believe a word he says, and he knows you don't. Nevertheless, for some mysterious reason the ritual has to be gone through every time anything changes hands at a reasonable price. The man who won't play simply won't get down to the just price. We have cut out most of that, but we still talk fatuously of a 'starting price' when we are offering a house for sale. I suppose a starting price is the price one just dares to hope the other fellow may turn out to be green enough to pay. If he *is* green, it seems to me it must be dishonest.

His greenness makes you a sort of trustee for him. If he is not green, then perhaps it's not dishonest — but — oh, how *silly* it is! God, what a way for a man that stands upright between the earth and sky to use the spirit that is in him!"

At this point I stopped abruptly and told Burden that I should like to go out somewhere into the air for a little.

"Out!" he snapped. "Certainly not! Caudle's due in five minutes. You know it!"

It was very hard luck that this particular client (the little, diddling usurer man who is so frightfully interested in his own affairs) should have chosen this particular day for his appointment. The very sound of his name, hearing it as I did just at the end of that long and irritating argument, fell on my ears like the last straw on the camel. And then something — something seemed to come *rushing up* inside me. Burden is always worrying about keeping clients. I, on the other hand, have spent many happy moments devising special methods of getting rid of them. What hundreds of ways one can think of! There was one in particular which I had long been anxious to try ...

"Mr. Caudle to see you, Sir!" said the office-boy.

"See him in a minute," said Burden automatically. He turned and glared at me. "Now," he said threateningly, "are you ready?"

I made no answer.

"Show Mr. Caudle in," said Burden down the telephone.

I fought down a hideous black, choking sensation; and then — I made my decision quickly. As I heard the handle of the door beginning to turn, I rose up, grasped the waste-paper basket and with a single swift movement inverted it over Burden's head, settling it well down on his shoulders. This took about a second. In another I had crossed the room to the door, snatching up a round black ruler as I went and keeping well clear of the draught to the chimney (*Hey, up the chimney-pot! Hey, after you!*), as I now no longer wanted to get out into the air.

I had just time for a fleeting glimpse of Burden sitting, like Marius amid the ruins of Carthage, under a sort of snow-storm of torn papers and envelopes, and then the door opened and the client came in. At the same moment I stepped smartly from behind it and brought the ruler down on the top of his bowler hat.

What happened after that I can't exactly say. It all seemed confused. I don't think Caudle said anything at first. But the whole thing is a jumble of impressions, from which the only ones that emerge clearly in my memory are of myself on my knees under the table, peering round one of the legs at Caudle and saying "Peek-a-bo!" with my head cocked archly on one side; of a struggle; of someone spluttering out "Gentlemen! *Gentlemen — please!*" in a tone midway between indignation and pained reproach; of another struggle by the open door, in which a ruler, a bowler-hat, a waste-paper basket and various heads and boots all figured. Then someone said: "Yes, I'm *quite* clear about the seven per cent interest," and then the door shut and I was sitting on the floor with my back against the wall, gasping for breath, and there was Burden sitting at his table quietly making a note in his diary as if nothing had happened.

"Burden!" I gasped in a weak, choking voice, "*Burden!*"

"Well?" He said.

"Did — did I really do all that?"

"Yes," he said sternly, "but *I* didn't."

*   *   *   *   *

It was that night the crisis came.

There is one advantage in having an inside that quivers like a jelly all the time. It enables you to make a systematic study of the condition. People talk of the courage of despair, but has anyone ever seriously investigated the relation between fear and will? I believe it is remarkably close. If over a fairly long period you dislike and shrink from nearly everything you have to do, you are also conscious of positively *willing* everything you do. Then, when you do get a chance to relax completely, this purely volitional self, reacting from the normal condition of strained exertion, makes itself felt in surprising ways. You find it is still there, though it is not doing anything — this mysterious unknown whose whole function is, precisely — *doing!*

Don't let me be misunderstood. I am not saying that your will necessarily becomes stronger, only that at such times you become very conscious of it. It upholds you; you seem to float on it as on a sort of buoyant, hyaline sea. You recognise the faint quivering of that sea, though it is no longer within you. "God," said Epictetus, "hath entrusted me with myself: He hath made my will subject to myself alone and given me rules for the right use thereof."[3] Can one imagine a more awe-inspiring discovery than this, that in doing so He entrusted me with *more* than myself?

Of course nothing of this sort takes place if Burden is so inconsiderate as to insist on accompanying me to bed. As a rule he only does so if we have both been working up to the last minute before retiring. But tonight he came for another reason. He had been angry all day since the scene with Caudle, and had hardly said a word. Now he came into the room, sat on the bed and said quietly: "I'm going to kill you."

I snatched up a heavy volume of *Paradise Lost* which I had by my bedside at the time.

"Two can play at that game!" I said, with my heart thumping against my ribs.

"Oh, don't be silly!" he sneered. "Not now, not violently. It will be gradual. I've begun already, as you know very well."

I wish I knew how to convey an impression of the depths I plumbed during the argument which followed these words. For they were true.

The conviction that they were true went through me like a sword, and seemed to leave me no strength to fight. I had no hope. Yet I could not succumb to a mere assertion and a mere threat.

---

[3] Epictetus, *Discourses*. "On Diligence" (Περὶ προσοχῆς) 4.12.

Mechanically I kept the conversation going. I began by telling him (without conviction) that he could not manage without me and he knew it. I enumerated all the things I did each day, in the Office and out of it, to help keep the practice going. But he took the ground away from under my feet. He was quite fair. He admitted them all, but said they were not essential.

"When I have finished killing you," he said, "there will be an end of all these idiotic arguments we keep having. That in itself, by freeing my attention, will be nearly as great a gain as all the losses you have been stressing. I don't deny there will be *some* loss. I shall have to give up some of the high-grade stuff that you bring in and attend to. But I can do without it. Incidentally it's not particularly paying! I shall do very well. I shall turn into a comfortable applejohn and end my days in conveyancing and peace."

I was silent for a long time. At last I thought of something to say.

"You won't be able to go on practising for ever," I said. "What about when you retire? What about when you die?"

I said this chiefly because I couldn't think of anything else to say. But the effect was surprising. Retirement didn't bother him at all. By that time he expected to have acquired the normal tastes of an applejohn and probably a hobby. Death, it seemed, was another matter.

I will not record the whole conversation. I pressed the point hard as soon as I perceived that it had touched him. It took a long time, and it was long before I felt any real hope of success. Yet, surprising as it sounds, I did in the end succeed in changing his purpose by the following flimsy argument. I convinced him that if *he* should survive *me*, then when in his turn he came to die, that most certainly would be the end. Whereas if I survived him, there at least *might*, even after my death, be something more. On this ground, and this alone, he reluctantly agreed to let me live on.

"Very well," he said, "I won't kill you. But I'll emasculate you. You shall be my eunuch. You will do what you are told in future. You will stop making suggestions of your own. And above all you will stop arguing."

But by this time I knew I had gained the upper hand, and this silly threat hardly caused me a tremor.

"I don't agree," I said. "If those are your terms, I shall commit *hara kiri*."

He gave in!

Shortly after this he left the room at my request. I had won one of the hardest battles of my life, and for a long time I lay quietly and peacefully in bed, thinking of all the other solicitors with sleeping partners like myself. For do not imagine that Burden is the only one. Applejohns dozing demurely after lunch, lynxes barking down their telephones, glossies in all the glory of their self-sufficiency, they are none of them without these *alter egos*. They would not be there without us. The very profession itself, and the law which it helps to administer, would not be there. For if it is the Burdens of this world who keep traditions alive, it is the Burgeons who create them. The Burdens cannot make anything; they can only collect and preserve.

And then I began to wonder drowsily if we Burgeons need always remain *sleeping* partners. Why should not we wake up sometimes and take a hand once more in the practice both of law and of life? And for a brief moment I fancied myself appealing, an impassioned orator, to my fellow Burgeons to do this very thing. But as I drew nearer to the sacred portals, I began already to dream. I dreamed that they had responded to the call. And the last thing I remember before falling sound asleep is, that I seemed to myself to hear the tramp of marching feet, and trumpets, and a tumult of shouting in the quiet precincts of Lincoln's Inn, while the long, dim corridors that lead from Carey Street to the Strand rang with the cries of *Sleepers awake!* and *Up, the Burgeons!*

When I awoke the next morning, I recalled with remarkable vividness not only this reverie-dream that I had had before falling asleep, but also two long and interesting deep-sleep dreams which perhaps grew out of it. I shall try to record them both before they fade.

X

HOME GUARD

(The First Dream)

"THE LEARNED JUDGE (the Lord Chancellor was saying) dismissed the Petition on the ground that he had no discretion to overlook the fact of the Petitioner's own adultery. The Court of Appeal unanimously upheld his decision, but granted leave to appeal to this House.

"Mr. Dawson (he went on) has sought to argue on behalf of the Appellant that, notwithstanding the matrimonial sections of the *Judicature Act* 1965,[1] the law has remained unaltered with respect to the Court's discretion to overlook a Petitioner's own matrimonial offences freely confessed. He says these are still a discretionary, not an absolute, bar to a decree. He admits that the statutory discretion conferred on the Court by Section 4 of the *Matrimonial Causes Act* 1937 has been removed following the repeal of that Section by the 1965 Act, but he says there is an inherent discretion at common law or by virtue of the principles of ecclesiastical law, which the Courts have recognised and adopted in the past in the exercise of their divorce jurisdiction. He has presented this argument with great force and skill, but he has failed to convince me."

(As these last words failed to produce either any despondency or any elation in my breast, I concluded my presence in the House of Lords was due to curiosity

---

[1] Note: *This Ever Diverse Pair* was written in the late 1940s.

rather than to any professional or personal interest in the proceedings.)

"As, notwithstanding previous decisions to the like effect in the Courts below, this is the first occasion (His Lordship went on) on which the point has been argued before your Lordships since the *Judicature Act* 1965 came into force; and as that Act effected great, not to say startling, changes in the law, it may be convenient if I adopt the somewhat unusual course of briefly reviewing the history of the law of matrimonial causes in this country before I give the reasons for the conclusion I have come to that this appeal must be dismissed.

"Marriage has never, or had never prior to 1965, been regarded as a contract between two parties in which none but the parties themselves were implicated. From earliest times the law has looked on it as a contract in which the whole of society is concerned, and has regarded its breach or observance as a matter touching the public interest. This is not surprising. It is obvious, for example, that when two people take the responsibility of bringing children into the world, that is a matter which concerns not merely themselves, but society as a whole. A family is a unit of society. Furthermore it was regarded as being more than a contract even *quoad*[2] the parties themselves. For marriage, besides creating a *relationship* between the parties, was looked on as altering, and altering irrevocably, the very parties themselves. It was not merely their system of contractual relationships which they varied

---

[2] With respect to.

when they bound themselves to one another, but their personal *status*.

"This Court is concerned with the law as it is and occasionally as it has been, not with public opinion or the way in which the law came to be. But in this instance what I have to say may be better understood if I remark in passing that until roughly the middle of the last century it was taken for granted that all marriages were permanent and indissoluble, and the law, reflecting this state of opinion, knew of no machinery for their dissolution. Prior to 1857, therefore, divorce *a vinculo matrimonii* could only be compassed by persuading the legislature to intervene with a special Act of Parliament. The *Matrimonial Causes Act* 1857 made it possible for a husband to pray for a dissolution of his marriage on the ground of his wife's adultery, and for a wife to divorce her husband for adultery coupled with certain aggravating circumstances. The *Matrimonial Causes Act* 1923 removed this distinction between husband and wife, and thereafter a dissolution could be prayed by either party on the sole ground of the adultery of the other.

"The next landmark is, of course, Herbert's Act — that is, the *Matrimonial Causes Act* 1937. It is noteworthy that the changes which it introduced were for the first time not wholly in the direction of easier divorce. While on the one hand it added several fresh grounds for dissolution, such as desertion and cruelty, yet on the other, inasmuch as it postponed the right of either spouse to pray for a dissolution for a period of three years from the date of the marriage, and by enjoining the Court to inquire more closely than before into the question of collusion, it may be said to have rendered divorce more difficult. In other words, the hitherto uniform development of the law on the subject was, as it were, rent asunder, and thereafter that development has continued in two divergent, perhaps opposite, directions.

"Between the years 1937 and 1965 there was no further change in the substantive law, but for the reasons I have stated it may not be amiss if I again draw attention to a group of facts which I should normally forbear, as being the province of the sociologist rather than the jurist. From the introduction of the 1923 Act the work of the Probate Divorce and Admiralty Division, as it was then called, began to increase to an extent probably never contemplated by the framers of that Act, still less by the framers of its predecessor of 1857. After Herbert's Act became law, the rate of increase continued to accelerate, partly because of the new grounds introduced by that Act, but much more, in my opinion, from the same causes which were operating previously, and which would have continued to operate even if the law had remained unchanged. I refer to the growth in numbers and influence of that section of the population which has come to regard marriage purely as a contract made for the convenience of the parties, and therefore one which should be terminable at any time by mutual consent. From the point of view of litigants so minded, and so consenting, the husband's adultery was still the easiest, the quickest and the cheapest ground on which a dissolution could be obtained, and the vast majority of suits continued to be brought on this ground, the evidence revealing in most cases that both parties concurred in desiring the dissolution. To use the common term, the majority of undefended cases continued to be 'hotel cases'.

"I am glad to take this opportunity of saying that the incident popularly known as the 'Solicitors' Strike' of 1952 has in my opinion been misnamed. It is true that a large number of solicitors refused for a time to practise in the Courts and proclaimed through an *ad hoc* representative body, set up without the approval of the Law Society, that they would have no more to do with what they termed 'the dirty business' until the law was changed. But solicitors are under no contract to accept clients' business, and this concerted action involved accordingly no breach of contractual duty such as we associate with an industrial strike. Moreover their demonstrations were conducted in the orderly manner which we should expect of a profession with venerable traditions. I myself happened to witness the procession round Lincoln's Inn Fields on the day on which the incident that finally led to the appointment of the Royal Commission of 1952 took place. I allude, of course, to the occasion when the President of the Probate Divorce and Admiralty Division, as it then was, having listened with his accustomed patience and courtesy to the 39th Undefended Case on the day's list, instead of stating whether he granted or refused a decree, rose from the Bench and, throwing his wig at one of His Majesty's Counsel then pleading at the Bar, left the Court and placed himself at the head of the procession.

"When the Royal Commission of 1952 concluded its investigations into the state of public opinion on the subject, it found that this was now sharply divided, having moved still further apart in the two divergent directions already adumbrated, as I have said, in Herbert's Act. On the one hand there was a large and clamant body of opinion which advocated the introduction of divorce by mutual consent, coupling with this a demand for the legalisation of abortion and other reforms of a progressive nature. On the other, there was a considerably larger, though less vocal, body which had either remained unaffected by the altered view of marriage reflected in the development of the law up to 1937 or had become more firmly convinced than before (possibly from observation of certain results which it attributed to that development) that marriage is essentially a social and a permanent institution. The two sections of opinion were opposed to one another almost diametrically; reconciliation proved impossible; and it was decided to embody the findings of the Commission, which were promulgated in 1957, in three separate statutes, the *Judicature Act* 1965, the *Marriage (Religious or Solemn Form) Act* 1965 and the *Marriage by Civil Contract Act* 1965.

"By Sections 95 to 100 of the *Judicature Act* 1965 the old Probate Divorce and Admiralty Division was abolished, the Matrimonial Division of the High Court established and practically the whole of the existing law of matrimonial causes was introduced for the first time. The two Marriage Acts altered, as is well known, the law of marriage itself.

"The marriage between the Petitioner and his wife, the Respondent, has subsisted for fifteen years, having been celebrated in 1966 — that is, after the Marriage Acts had come into force. Counsel for the Petitioner has pressed very hard that the refusal of a decree must not only involve great hardship, but must also be contrary to the public interest where one of the parties at all events has 'lost all affection', as he says, for the other. No Answer was filed on behalf of the Respondent, and it may well be that her feelings have undergone a similar change. We do not know.

"The particulars of the Petitioner's marriage with the Respondent are quite properly set forth in the Petition, and it is not disputed that this is a 'marriage of status' within the *Marriage (Religious or Solemn Form) Act* 1965. Whatever the hardship involved, your Lordships are of course bound to apply the law as it stands. Let us none the less examine for a moment how much of justification underlies this plea. As younger people, the Petitioner and the Respondent could, if they had chosen, have entered into a 'marriage of contract' under the *Marriage by Civil Contract Act* 1965. That marriage would have enjoyed the full protection of the law. The Respondent would have been entitled to join her name to the Petitioner's by a hyphen, without either of them executing any deed or document, and all the provisions of the Act as to property, income-tax and the wife's inalienable right to salary as a house-keeper would have applied. Evidence of their co-habitation would have afforded no defence to an action brought by either of them against a third party for defamation of character by alleging immoral behaviour. Their children would have been legitimate. Nevertheless the marriage could at any time have been dissolved on proof of any of the numerous offences specified in Section 130 of the *Judicature Act* 1965 or, with the consent of both parties, without any legal proceedings at all — merely by their making a joint Declaration and attending before a Magistrate in his private room. The only restriction to which they would have been subject would have been that they could not resort to this last remedy within one year from the date of the marriage, and that the number of their subsequent marriages with other parties would have been limited to one in any one period of twelve months, and to a total of six in all. True, they would also have been subject to the disability that neither party could ever afterwards have entered into a 'marriage of status' either with the original spouse or with any subsequent one. As far as the original spouse is concerned, this can hardly be called a restriction, since the rights of dissolution given by the *Marriage by Civil Contract Act* are of course permissive only, and not obligatory. As far as a subsequent spouse is concerned, the very idea of the co-existence of two spouses is repugnant to a 'marriage of status' as defined by the Act which enables it.

"They deliberately chose not to avail themselves of these facilities. The Acts were widely publicised, and it must have been with their eyes open that the parties to this suit elected to enter into a marriage of status with one another fifteen years ago. The interval of three months which the 'Solemn Form' Act fixes between the notification and the celebration of such marriages gave them ample time not only to reflect on the spiritual meaning of the vows which they proposed to take, but also to investigate in detail their practical consequences. Since then they and their children have enjoyed all the advantages which flow from such a choice. The Respondent, for instance, has been entitled to the dignity — the *gravitas* [3] if I may use the word — which attaches to the honourable title of 'Mrs'. Her children have grown up in the atmosphere of a home. Moreover, birds of a feather flock together, and I make no doubt that both parties have had the entrée to pleasant circles in which the adults know who is alluded to when anyone mentions this man's 'wife' or that woman's 'husband', and where the children take it for granted that the wife in any household is the mother and the husband the father. They chose to tread, and they have trodden, the solid ground of lives governed by principle rather than caprice, and guided by a steady resolve through the veering gusts of egotism and passion. They have breathed the fresh air of mutual ease and confidence which blows over those pleasant regions, encompassing even their parched and rocky tracts with a climate of grace. They have had the freedom of the city of constancy and self-control. Their children have played and waxed in strength behind its sheltering walls, instead of ripening to precocious maturity in the fugitive

---

[3] The Roman term *gravitas* implies more than mere dignity; it is a compendium of respectability, solidity, and authority.

encampments of the so-called companionate marriages. In my opinion they cannot now withhold their scot and lot either in honour or in law. The very existence of that city depends on the fact that their marriage, as part of a network of such marriages throughout the realm, not only was, but was always publicly known to be a life-marriage. The defence of that city against the siege which has been laid to it was clearly one of the objects which the legislature had in mind in enacting the *Marriage (Religious or Solemn Form) Act* 1965. Because a man *was* a volunteer, it does not follow that he is entitled to *be* a deserter. The Petitioner cannot therefore be heard to say now that after all a life-marriage was not what he wanted. At least he cannot be heard to say it except in circumstances of the utmost gravity, and upon the unalterable condition that he himself comes into Court with clean hands.

"Mr. Dawson suggests that a choice made so long ago cannot be binding, and that the Petitioner should now be free to start again. But this would be to stultify the whole principle of election which the Marriage Acts introduced. For not to claim this freedom was the very thing which the parties elected to do. They laid it, so to speak, as a burnt-offering on the altar of household gods, and they and their children and friends have breathed the incense which mingled with the smoke of the sacrifice. Now, fifteen years later, the Petitioner seeks to aver through his Counsel that the offering was never consumed at all. It will not do.

"In short, there is nothing in what Mr. Dawson has said that tempts me to place a strained construction on the words of the *Judicature Act* 1965. In construing a Statute the natural sense of the words must be taken unless the result is inherently preposterous or unreasonable. I have shown that, so far from its being preposterous, the plain meaning of Section 121 of the *Judicature Act* 1965 is in my opinion eminently reasonable. I hold therefore that the learned Judge was right in holding that he had no discretion to overlook the fact of the Petitioner's own adultery, and the Appeal fails on that ground.

"I may add that, on the evidence disclosed to your Lordships, there is another objection to this Petition which would have been fatal to its success, even had there been no such bar. It is founded on a single act of adultery alleged to have been committed by the Respondent with an unnamed man. The Petitioner must surely have been advised that since 1965 that is quite insufficient. In order to succeed, he would have to show that the Respondent persisted in her infidelity to an extent which raises a presumption that her true will has changed; so that she has not merely strayed under temptation into a casual breach of the marriage oath, but has in effect repudiated it. There is not nearly enough in the evidence on the record to raise such a presumption.

"My advice to the Petitioner is to go away and think again. The old suit for Restitution of Conjugal Rights has long been abolished, and the Court will take no step, either of its own accord or on the motion of either party to compel him and the Respondent to live together. Nevertheless I advise him to think again and to consult with the Respondent again. If, after they have done so, it is still the fixed and settled conviction of either party that his home cannot be re-established, either of them can go back to the learned Judge of the Matrimonial Division, who tried their cause in the first instance. He will then in the exercise of the equitable jurisdiction in infants' matters transferred to him from the Chancery Division, hear the views of both husband and wife, and assist them to find the arrangement next best calculated to secure the welfare of their infant children.

"My Lords, for the reasons which I have stated I am of the opinion that this Appeal should be dismissed with costs both here and below, and I move your Lordships accordingly."

XI

ASTRAEA REDUX[1]

(The Second Dream)

"—— IN HIS COURT of Star Chamber." There were only two Judges this time, and it was the one on the right who was delivering his judgment. 'These judges are getting very jurisprudence-minded,' I thought; and then I settled down again to listen. "That was the only attempt made prior to the *Criminal Sentences (Equitable Jurisdiction) Act* 1990[2] to introduce the principles of equity into the administration of criminal law.

"The principles of equity have not changed," His Lordship went on, "but the development throughout the last 400 years of another branch of the law altogether, namely the law of the Constitution, has introduced important new considerations affecting the application of those principles. The Lord Chancellor's jurisdiction (which in this country is another name for equity) was originally founded, and it still rests, on his quasi-royal function as keeper of the King's conscience; the King as *parens patriae* being responsible for the welfare, both physical and moral, of all his subjects. It is true, however, that the place occupied by the Crown itself in

---

[1] Latin. Lit. Astraea returned. The virgin goddess Astraea, a personification of Justice, was said by Ovid (*Met.* 1.149) to have left the world behind during the Age of Iron. Virgil (*Ecl.* 6.34) wrote of her return as the harbinger of a new Golden Age.

[2] Note: *This Ever Diverse Pair* was written in the late 1940s.

the structure of the Constitution has changed. It has been well settled for more than a hundred and fifty years past that the paramountcy of the Crown derives from its representing, not the personal will of the sovereign but the sovereign will of the people. It follows that the Lord Chancellor today is not the keeper of one man's conscience but the keeper of the consciences of the people as a whole, of those very people who are subject to his jurisdiction. Now, the conscience cannot, by its nature, be compelled or bound by rules imposed *ab extra*. It is itself the rule-maker, whether that making be by new invention or by free acknowledgment and submission. It was the recognition of this voluntary principle by the Legislature which led to the two great changes introduced by the *Criminal Sentences (Equitable Jurisdiction) Act*, 1990.

"The first of these changes was of course the extension of the principles of equity from civil to criminal causes. The second was that principle of voluntary submission to which I have already alluded. A court of equity is a court of conscience. It proceeds on the principle that the conscience of the wrongdoer must be purged by *making* restitution rather than on the principle that the wronged party has a 'right' to receive it. Now, in civil causes, lying between two parties, it was considered unjust to deprive the sufferer of those equitable remedies which had been established by long usage, so as to make *them* dependent on the voluntary submission of the wrongdoer. In criminal matters, on the other hand, it was clear that the conscience of the guilty party was still the first consideration. Accordingly it was provided by the Act of

1990 that the equitable jurisdiction in the matter of criminal sentences which the Act conferred could only be exercised over those who, after verdict given against them, had voluntarily submitted themselves to it. Failing such submission, their punishment, or other treatment, is still determined according to the law as it stood before the introduction of the Act.

"I ought perhaps to add that the *Judicature Act* 1990, which provided that judicial precedents should no longer be binding on any court so far as concerns the application of equitable principles, applies to *all* jurisdiction in equity, whether in civil or criminal matters. Previously the growth of an immense volume of case law, obscuring the distinction between law and equity, had almost obliterated that more elastic and human quality which, in its origin, had been regarded as equity's especial virtue, and as the very foundation of its claim to override the ruthless logic of the common law."

It was at about this point in his Lordship's judgment that I began to feel vaguely uneasy. I say vaguely, because what worried me most, as so often in dreams and fevers, was that I could not exactly fix *what* it was that worried me. What was it? Somehow the Court *looked* wrong. It was the wrong shape. What, I kept asking myself, was amiss with it?

Then things began to grow clearer to me. There was nothing wrong with the Court. It was I who was wrong. Or rather my position. I was seeing it from an unaccustomed angle! And almost simultaneously the whole truth burst in on me. I was in the dock! Yes, in the dock; and there, sitting dejectedly beside me, was my partner.

It must have happened at last then. *Re a Solicitor!* How often had Burden and I read that ominous heading above the little paragraphs in the *Law Society's Gazette* which tell of brothers who have fallen by the way. And now we too must have slipped up somehow. For us too, no doubt, the little paragraph had appeared, to be followed, after the erasure of our names from the honourable Roll of Solicitors, by a criminal prosecution.

Suddenly, as the full implications of this thought were borne in on me, my heart leaped. Off the Rolls! Free at last! Did anything else matter? Oh, I realised of course that I had as yet no idea what was coming to me; but at least it would be real life. A stern enough problem, perhaps, but at least something worth tackling in earnest: an altogether new technique of living to acquire. Even a convict's existence must offer *these* things — *and there would be no responsibilities!* It was as if a huge half-forgotten weight had been lifted from my spirits and for a moment they rocketed to unimaginable heights and began to dance there. I was almost too excited to listen to what was being said. Had it been less novel and interesting, I doubt if I should have heard a word, except what concerned my own fate. But it *was* interesting. English criminal law had evidently been altered in several remarkable ways since I had last had anything to do with it. Sentence, for example, was apparently being passed in a different Court from that in which the verdict had been given. How Burden and I came to be living in the

1990's did not trouble me at all. I never even considered it. But in a dream there is no knowing what natural things will appear strange or what strange things natural.

Meanwhile the Judge was continuing his exposition of the law as it stood in the last decade of the twentieth century. "Both prisoners," he said, "have chosen to submit themselves to the jurisdiction of this Court. Had they chosen differently, they would have been dealt with by the Court which tried them and found them guilty. That Court would have had the advantage of the clear Statutory enactments, which deal with the treatment of criminals. In view of the abolition of retributive punishment in 1976, it must have directed them to receive medical and psychological treatment at the hands of the State Institute of Criminology, which, as they well know, proceeds on the assumption that crime is a form of disease, for which the criminal is in no way responsible, and that right and wrong are terms descriptive merely of healthy and unhealthy reactions to external stimuli. Instead, they have chosen the course provided by the Statute of 1990 for those who prefer the voluntary acceptance of personal responsibility to the alternative of compulsory treatment. According to the record, the prisoner Burden stated, in making his election, that he 'would not have any damned witch-doctor meddling with his glands'. We think he might have expressed himself with greater moderation, but we have no doubt that he was wise in his choice.

"The difficulties which this Court has to face in the exercise of this still somewhat novel jurisdiction do not need to be stressed by me. The greatest of them is that we, being ourselves fallible and sinful human beings, are bound to award the penalty which in our opinion will most benefit the free will and heal the soul of the prisoner before us. In other words, we must attempt to make decisions of a kind which our forefathers believed lay exclusively within the province of Almighty God, working through destiny. I need hardly say that we approach such a task with the deepest humility. We should not dare to undertake it at all but for two reflections which support us in our deliberations. The first of these is the fact that prisoners who come before us for sentence do so in some degree voluntarily. All those who entrust us with their purgation were free, if they preferred it, to let the common law take its course. The second is the fact that it is the function of a judge merely — to judge. In exercising his authority he does not rely on any superior merit presumed in himself, but solely on the principles of justice and equity in which he has been trained. The observation of Lord Coleridge in the case of *Rex* v. *Dudley and Stephens* is apt to the point here. That was a case in which two of three shipwrecked sailors, starving in an open boat, had killed and eaten the third. In sentencing these two to death for the crime of murder, Lord Coleridge remarked, apropos of the terrible nature of the temptation to which these unfortunate men had been exposed: –

> "'We are often compelled to set up standards we cannot reach ourselves, and to lay down rules which we could not ourselves satisfy. But a man has no right to declare temptation to be an excuse even though he might himself have yielded to

it, nor allow compassion for the criminal to change or weaken in any manner the legal definition of the crime.'

It is not therefore impossible, though in this Court it may be peculiarly difficult, for an indifferent man to be a wise judge even of a better one.

"Turning to the two cases now before us, I propose to deal first with the prisoner Burden. The Court is of the opinion that he is a man of normally steady character without either great ambitions or great ideals. It required, we believe, a temptation out of the common course to make him fall. But we find that he is too fond, not exactly of pleasure, but of the ordinary external comforts of a temperate life: good meals, health, warmth, a comfortable bed at night — in a word, security. He lacks the inner strength which was needed to make him face with resolution the risk of losing these things, or some of them. We are further of the opinion that this lack of inner strength is connected with the general temper of his mind. It is a quick and accurate mind, but without the leaven of imagination. It does not readily soar. He enjoys, and enjoys keenly, intellectual activity of a forensic or even dialectical nature. Precision in thought and in expression give him pleasure, and in that respect the prisoner is well suited to his profession of the law. But there are other qualities of the mind besides agility and precision. Our task is to consider what is needed by the whole man in order to make him truly whole. We have to ask ourselves what will right the balance which events have shown to be unstable.

"We think that a sharp change in his way of life for some time to come will provide an appropriate purgation, and we have decided on the precise nature of that change. We have consulted with the Purgation Officer, and he has informed us of a household which the prisoner will join and where he will remain until a further order is made. It is a household in which the parents are both in poor health and are, through lack of means, without any of the domestic help which they badly need. His working day will be occupied with the menial tasks (other than cooking) incident to a family of five. He will sleep hard, rise early and dress rough. In such free time as is at his disposal no restriction will be placed on his attending concerts, dramatic performances and other public entertainments, but the books which he will be allowed to read will be subject to supervision for some time to come. He will have a choice, but it will be a restricted choice. They will, for instance, not include detective stories or the works of P. G. Wodehouse. It is, however, not anticipated that the prisoner will have a large amount of time available for private reading. The three young children in the family are all fond of fairy-tales, and it will be part of the prisoner's duties to read aloud to them and after a time to endeavour to narrate to them *ex tempore*[3] similar stories of his own invention. I should add that the lady of the house, whose eyesight is weak, is interested in literature of a fanciful and vaguely mystical description. The Purgation Officer has taken the trouble to ascertain her

---

[3] *Ex tempore*. Lat. Without preparation or forethought; on the spur of the moment.

plans for the immediate future, and the prisoner will spend a good part of his evenings, after the children have gone to bed, in reading aloud to this lady the *Prophetic Books of William Blake*, the *Oxford Book of Mystical Verse*, the *Mabinogion*, and the writings both in prose and in verse of *Fiona Macleod*.

"The case of the prisoner Burgeon," went on the Judge, "presents some rather more difficult features."

I stiffened slightly and became more attentive. But even now I cannot say that I felt apprehensive, only rather excited. As I am somewhat introspective by nature, and am moreover constantly finding myself involved in small but apparently insoluble moral problems, I often actually look forward to the inevitable interview with Rhadamanthus:[4] not by any means because I think my choices have generally been right, but rather in the same way that a man who has tried and failed to solve a chess-problem looks forward to the appearance of the journal containing the authoritative solution. When I reflect that, whatever else that dread judgment contains, it must at least disclose the right answers to all my bewildering problems, I can hardly help believing that I shall be too much interested to be afraid. Fortified with this complacent view of the Last Judgment itself, it is not surprising if I now prepared myself with some indulgence to hear anything which a mere earthly tribunal might have to say.

"We find," said the Judge, "that he is in many ways, and by the world's standards, a man of exceptionally high

[4] In Greek mythology, Rhadamanthus is a judge of the souls of the dead. He was awarded this role because of his exemplary integrity.

character. He is certainly no egoist. *He* is not unduly attached to his comforts, and we can well believe that he would sacrifice them and much else for the welfare of others, if ever the occasion for doing so presented itself to him in a perfectly clear light. We are less sure that any occasion would ever in fact so present itself. Moreover, he is gifted with considerable mental powers, and these are by no means of the somewhat earthbound quality which we detected in the case of his fellow-prisoner."

I nearly yawned. If this was all he had to say, I might as well have stayed away. It was the things I had done *wrong* that I wanted to hear about, not the things I knew I had done right. The latter, I felt, I could make a fair shift to enumerate for myself.

"On the contrary," His Lordship continued, "he has a mind which is capable of soaring. In fact," he added with severity, "we are of the opinion that it soars rather too easily — like a balloon."

I became more interested. It didn't hurt, mind; for, with the assistance of certain obliging friends, I had more than once received an inkling of this foible already.

"We find nothing in the profession which he has adopted," the Judge went on, "which should encourage this defect. The necessity of deciding doubtful questions and of acting immediately on the decisions instead of continuing happily to speculate about them, the precision of thought which the study of the law demands and the constant exercise which it affords in the dry process of detecting dissimilarities between principles which are exceedingly — and for a man of his temperament, perhaps excitingly — similar — all these things should have exerted, and must in the long run exert, a highly beneficial influence. But there is something more.

"We find that the prisoner is highly sensitive to the outer surface of the sphere of human fellowship. He loves to be on good terms with everybody. He cannot bear the slightest suggestion of harshness in his personal relationships, even where these are of a casual or superficial nature. What it must mean to him when such occurs in connections of a deeper kind, it would be difficult to imagine."

(Very good. But why had the Judge's tone remained so severe now that he was reverting to my merits? My well-known good-humour — people think it comes quite naturally to me. So it does *now*, but only as the result of persevering efforts in the distant past.)

"We can conceive of circumstances in which he would readily damage himself, but would not have the firmness to damage another, even though the occasion clearly demanded it — especially if he knew that in doing so he must incur that other's hostility, resentment or reproaches."

Really, this was getting absurd! So unwillingness to hurt people was a vice, was it? I began to feel justifiably angry — angry with the coolly pontificating Judge, angry with the Court and the whole newfangled system of criminal equity.

"He is a happy warrior in a pure conflict of wits," the Judge continued inexorably, "but he shrinks violently — more violently than perhaps he knows — from anything approaching a conflict of wills. Almost equally so, whether the opposing will be weaker or stronger than his own. It was, we believe, in an effort to evade precisely such a conflict (and not a very serious one) that he lapsed into dishonesty, at first with himself, and afterwards with others. Rather than hurt anybody's feelings, and have perhaps to meet an angry or a wounded look, he was prepared to pretend that things were not as they were. He did so. Once having begun, he could not stop without a still sharper conflict. He went on doing so. And so he fell."

The Judge paused, removed his glasses, held them for a moment at arm's length on the table in front of him and replaced them on his nose as he continued: –

"We have given very anxious consideration to this case, and I am glad to say that we are in complete accord in the conclusion we have come to. We have reviewed many possible alterative courses, but having done so, we are both agreed that, whether from the point of view of purgation strictly so called, by the suffering which it will inevitably entail, or from a purely remedial point of view, by the faculties which it must call forth and the exertions which it must demand, we can direct nothing better for this prisoner than that he ..."

I was holding my breath now:

"Should continue to practise as a solicitor until further Order. He will, of course, bear the additional weight of sole responsibility until such time as his partner, having as we hope been purged of his offence, returns to practise with him. For the protection of his clients the Court will appoint a supervisor who will countersign all cheques for the first six months, but we hope and believe that this is more a matter of form than of necessity, and that he will carry the heavier load which we are placing on his shoulders more surely and steadily than the lighter one beneath which he formerly stumbled."

It was the end for me — the end of all my excitement and of all my eager interest in the new system of criminal equity, even the end of my anger and resentment. I had thought, in my over-weening self-confidence, that I had the spiritual strength to meet with rejoicing anything that the Court could devise for me. But their devising was more skilful than I had imagined, and it seemed I had nothing to meet *this* with. The balloon had been pricked and, after the inglorious fashion of its kind, it collapsed. The next case was called.

And then — just before I turned to leave the Court with lowered head and leaden steps — for a brief instant, above the row of white pigtails and rustling papers my eyes met those of the presiding Judge. It was he who had been delivering judgment, and I saw at once why he had been chosen for his work. It is true the whole thing was only a dream, but I fancy I shall lose many vivid impressions of my waking life before I forget — before I forget that pregnant moment in which the countenance of Equity looked into my countenance and the soul of Equity pierced calmly to the naked worm at the core of this uneasily bombinating soul and *yet* seemed to welcome it gladly as a brother!

* * * * *

I see that firm, kindly face as clearly before me now as I did when I awoke on the following morning. It was that more than anything else, I believe, which enabled me to achieve, and it is that which enables me to maintain the better understanding which now exists between Burden and myself. I have apologised to him for losing my head so disgracefully over the Caudle incident, and he has withdrawn all his threats, and shows by his conduct that he knows his place. As a result the whole *modus operandi* of the partnership has been greatly improved. We have even worked out its application to details — such as our collaboration in the drafting of affidavits.

By the same token there is, sad to say, no longer any reason to go on writing this 'diary', as I have not very accurately called it. It has helped us both through a difficult period, and now it has served its turn, and the need is past. Good-bye to it, then. It began shortly after the only occasion in which Burden appeared to me in a dream. It is fitting that it should close here at the end of the only dream in which he *disappeared* from me. For this last one did not fade until I had caught a final glimpse of the bowler hat moving off, not without dignity, in the direction of the Brixton villa in which its occupant had been directed by the Court to hew the wood of simplicity and draw the water of imagination. As for myself, I turned my face grimly towards the Office. And the effort of doing so awoke me with a jerk.

SELECTED WORKS BY OWEN BARFIELD

First published

Books by Owen Barfield

Translations and edited works of Rudolf Steiner

Edited works by other authors